RUNAWAY SOUTHERN BELLE

A novel
by
Jerry L. Minshall

Zephyr Bulletin Press
Nashville, Tennessee

The story contained in these pages is fiction. Any reference to people who actually lived, events which actually happened, or places which are real on God's green earth, are used fictitiously.

RUNAWAY SOUTHERN BELLE

copyright ©2011

Jerry L. Minshall

Zephyr Bulletin Press

Nashville, Tennessee

Printed in the United States of America.

ISBN: 978-0-9981522-6-4

Cover Photo: Stan Walls
Model: J. D. Parker

also by
Jerry L. Minshall:

FLEEING CAT SPRING
The Texas Special Escape

SANTA FE COCKTAIL

To
R. C. "Bob" and Joyce

PROLOGUE

My name is Alben …and I am now a lady approaching her eightieth birthday. You cannot know how unrealistic that sounds to me—but it is true. I merely want to set down on paper a little of my life, before my memory fades. Perhaps my story might be helpful—at least interesting— to my descendants. I would say to those descendants, please stick with the story to the very end.

Now. I think I will be more comfortable, telling the story as an observer; the third person, rather than in the first person.

So. Let's see. How to begin?…perhaps with a little poem:

"…a folly so reckless…
…a foolish young fling…
…a selfish indulgence…
…brings others much pain…"

CHAPTER ONE
Conspiracy

Heavener, Oklahoma—
Thursday, January 20, 1949—
8:50 a.m.

The letter had arrived two days ago, and Miss Alben James Barkley (yes, it is Miss Barkley), now reads the letter for the seventh time. They have planned the daring escapade for months, the date set in stone a few days ago. And tonight is the night. The letter is just to encourage her to follow through. Not to chicken out at the last minute.

Alben had met Petty Officer 3rd Class Joey J. Thibodeaux last summer when he came to visit his aunt and cousin in Heavener. He had just turned twenty-two; was cute, Cajun, and a little wild. He was six-feet-one, wiry, complexion a little light to have such dark hair and eyes. Joey had "re-upped" after his first hitch, and still had three years to go before discharge from the United States Navy. He was an electrician in "this man's navy," and was now being reassigned from the naval shipyard in Long Beach, California to the Portsmouth Naval Shipyard, on Seavey's Island—Kittery, Maine. Seavey's Island was in the middle of the Piscatagua River. Ocean scientists determined years ago, the island's location and its rapid tidal currents, blocked winter's ice from closing off navigation, into and from, the Atlantic Ocean. Which made it perfect for a naval base.

"We build subs at Portsmouth," Joey told an enchanted Alben. She loved the way he looked in his white uniform. And the way he wore the little round cap, cocked at a jaunty angle on the right side of his forehead.

"You build what?" The starstruck Alben didn't know what the sailor was talking about.

"Subs," he repeated. "Submarines. That's what the U. S. Navy builds at Portsmouth."

"Oh," Alben responded, a little embarrassed. "Sorry. I didn't understand…what you meant." She paused. "You're so …so enthused. About the Navy, I mean. Ya gonna be a sailor all your life?"

"Don't know. Haven't decided. Got a little time yet to make that decision."

When Petty Officer Thibodeaux got started on the United States Navy it was difficult to stop him. He told Alben (until her eyes glazed over), there was this huge historic dispute whether the Portsmouth Naval Yard was actually in Maine, or New Hampshire. But somewhere in that conversation, Joey noticed the 'eye glaze,' and stopped lecturing …and resumed flirting.

"Ya gotta mighty pretty town, here. This Heavener, Oklahoma." He pronounced it HEH-vuhn-er.

Alben giggled. "We call it HEEV-ner 'round here," she said.

"Oh," he replied, a sheepish look on his face.

Joey had a three-week leave and got off the Rock Island Railroad's Golden State Limited in Kansas City, and hitchhiked down to Heavener to see some relatives. Alben had loved the way Joey looked at her from across the pavilion the first night she saw him. It was a summer dance in the park. His eyes moved up and down her body. He was looking at her that way every time she sneaked a peek his way. He finally came over to talk. His hometown was Rodessa, Louisiana—near Shreveport—and he'd been no place at all except Rodessa, Shreveport, New Orleans, and Beaumont, Texas. Until… he joined the navy. Now he had the cocky air of a world traveler.

Joey teased Alben about her name from the start. It was just a couple of days later at Scribner's Soda Shop: "Alben?? James??" he cracked. "They both sound like boy's names to me. Hell! My middle name is James." He paused, with a leering little grin. "But you sure don't look like no boy."

Sitting on a fountain barstool, Alben thought it the perfect moment to confirm Joey's macho declaration. She crossed her legs and tugged at the hem of her form-fitting, red skirt, as though moving it downward. The skirt moved not at all. Just as she intended. Then, she cocked one leg so the hem actually slid up. Well above her knees. She sat there, swinging that high heel shoe in a slow dangle, back and forth. Just like the Hollywood bombshells in the movies. She had dressed up that day because her summer Home Ec club was serving appetizers for the Ladies Auxillary of the American Legion.

"I ain't no boy," she said softly, a confident, even daring look on her face. "Alben is my great-uncle's name, and James is my mother's maiden name." She shrugged dramatically, hoping she mimicked Ava Gardner. "My parents named me. Whatevvvuh then, can I do?" Alben realized she had just sounded more like Scarlett O'Hara than Ava Gardner.

"Just what you're doin' now," Joey replied with a tender smile. "For 'bout three thousand forevers. That'd be just fine by me."

Before Alben knew what was happening, Joey reached into a duffel bag setting on the barstool next to him and pulled out a small, black box camera. He immediately snapped her picture. "I've never seen a camera like that," she laughed. The lettering said 'New York World's Fair' immediately below the lens.

"Got it in Beaumont," Joey replied. "Visiting an aunt on my fifteenth birthday, and she gave it to me. She went to the big fair in '39—bought three of 'em. That's the only place you could get 'em."

"You must've been her special pet," Alben teased. "Did you flirt with her too?"

Joey merely smiled and snapped three more shots. "I always carry it with me," he said, "just for times like this. "

"And I'll bet there are plenty of those!" Alben chided. There was a hint of jealousy in her tone.

Now, Alben tucked the letter safely in an inner pocket of her purse, slipped out of her shorty nightgown and panties, checked to make sure her bedroom door was locked, took the curlers from her long chestnut hair and began brushing it out in front of the dresser mirror. She had once read a blurb in a Hollywood movie magazine, that female stars of the silver screen often brushed their hair in front of a mirror, while nude. Something about a woman gaining confidence by seeing her own body unclothed. Who would've thought?

And Alben needed confidence right now. If the plan she and Joey had contrived was to be successful, she must appear at ease; perfectly normal. Calm, confident, casual. But the tremulous feeling in the pit of her stomach bore no resemblance to those terms.

CHAPTER TWO
Do I Dare?

10:37 a.m. —

The voices of the news announcers and analysts had been droning away loudly on the living room radio, a floor-model Stromberg-Carslon. Alben had heard the monotonous sound since waking up:

"...thousands of people in the streets of Washington, D. C. today..." "...of one thing you can be sure: for every thousand people here, 999 thought that Thomas Dewey and Earl Warren would be sworn in today, but 'Give 'em hell Harry' won it after all..." "...the new vice-president is Alben Barkley of Kentucky. At 71, he'll become the oldest vice-president in U. S. history..."

In Heavener, there's a much younger Alben Barkley—this girl, with the middle name of James. She's the great-niece of the new vice-president, and turns sixteen-and-a-half this very day. She has never met her great-uncle. But she's heard plenty about him for as long as she can remember. Alben—the Heavener, Oklahoma teenager—finishes brushing her luxurious chestnut hair around a photogenic face. Her light olive skin is flawless; her eyes, a brilliant deep blue. She thinks she has movie star looks (and does), and wishes she'd been born in Hollywood. Maybe she would have been one of those girls discovered for the silver screen at that famous Schwab's Drugstore on Sunset Boulevard. She knew about that from *Glamour of Hollywood* magazine.

By now, Alben has had quite enough of the news broadcasts. She unlocks and opens her bedroom door. "Momma," she calls downstairs, "would you please turn on some music?"

"No, child. There's none to be found anywhere. They're all broadcastin' the inauguration." And in a quiet aside to Mrs. Overton, young Alben's mother confides, "She's just like every sixteen-year-old girl! Music, makeup, and boys. Music, makeup, and boys! And do you hear the sug-ges-tive words in those hit parade songs?! My lord!!"

Mrs. Overton is the neighbor next door, here for her regular cup of mid-morning coffee. "Doesn't she understand it's her great-uncle who's becomin' Vice-President?" she asks.

"Oh… I think so… but, you know. She's just too young to care. "

"Momma," Alben calls again from her bedroom, "did you say you need butter and eggs? I'll be happy to drive to the store for you." Alben knows she needs to buy her train ticket before noon. That's when the new ticket agent of the Kansas City Southern Railway gets off. All the other agents know Alben, and would ask too many questions. They might even call her mother or father.

"That would be nice, dear," Mrs. Barkley responded. "But hurry. I want you to hear your great-uncle sworn in. The new Ford has a great radio."

Alben slipped into her new white blouse; the one with frilly lace on each side of the buttons. And tugged on her old blue and white plaid skirt––a little tight in just the right places. Her mother bought her the skirt when Alben was in the eighth grade.

"Take that thing to the Salvation Army," Mrs. Barkley constantly nagged. "Good gosh, you've grown six inches! It's no longer stylish. And! It's too short for a girl your age. "

"Maybe that's the reason I wear it, Momma." That's what Alben wanted to say, but did not. She'd wear her long, bright red winter coat today—a Christmas gift just last month from her parents—so her mother wouldn't see the skirt. A red wool winter hat—a tam, really—crisp white anklets, and shiny, black and white saddle shoes would complete her outfit.

"Oh, pretty Alben!" Mrs. Overton chirped when Alben entered the kitchen, "I love that new red coat. "

"Here's a twenty," said Mrs. Barkley, "better fill the Ford up. It's 'bout outa gas. Don't forget—I want the large brown eggs; and get a pound of Braum's Premium butter. And bring back my change!"

As Alben walked out the front door, Fred the Dog came bounding from his doghouse at the edge of the porch. "Hi, boy. Hi, puppy," she cooed reaching down to pet the twelve-week-old canine. "Back, Fred the Dog," Alben added, "back." The pup was already good at obeying commands, and scurried back to his doghouse—but whined all the way. "I don't want to run over you, baby," Alben called as she unlocked the car.

Fred the Dog was Mrs. Barkley's dog, recently acquired from a couple with a five-year-old boy, who had moved. They lived three doors down the street from the Barkleys, but were moving to Denver, and said they did not want to travel with a dog; that they'd get their son another one when they got settled in their new home.

"His name is Fred the Dog," said the sad boy. The pup was a snow white Labrador-Lancashire Heeler mix, with only a trace of black on one ear, a trace of tan on the other. The lad didn't merely call the dog Fred; he called him 'Fred the Dog'. Mrs. Barkley thought the kid was so cute and precious to speak so seriously, so matter-of-fact about it, she had also taken to calling the pup Fred the Dog. "I don't think he'll run off," said the boy, "since we're leaving his doghouse with you."

"We'll take real good care of Fred the Dog," Mrs. Barkley told the boy. "And anytime you visit from Denver, you can play with him all you want." That gave some comfort to the kid, since he was too young to know it was unlikely he'd ever set foot in Heavener, Oklahoma again.

Alben carefully backed the new car from the driveway. It was a '49 Ford Custom Club Coupe. She loved to drive her mom's new car and wanted never to risk the privilege by putting the slightest scratch on it. But now, it suddenly occurred: perhaps she'd never drive the Ford again! After today. That made her sad. And it made her more sad, when she thought of leaving Fred the Dog.

Alben had been very happy her dad bought the silver blue coupe. She thought it much more stylish than a sedan. Just right for a young girl who tried very hard to look like Ava Gardner. And that wasn't all that hard for Alben. She had the same Grecian lines to the cheek and jaw bones, the naturally dark, thick eyebrows and lashes. She even tried wearing her hair up on top her head, like Ava did in *One Touch Of Venus*. But it took too much time. Ava's look in long wavy hair was easier for Alben to mimic. Her own chestnut hair, put up in curlers for awhile then brushed out, worked well with an occasional trip to the beauty shop for a light perm.

Joey Thibodeaux was not the first boy to have trouble keeping his eyes off Alben. That had been a part of her life for the past three or four years. It had come to be a game at Scribner's Soda Shop after school. Each evening, around five, the mournful whistle of the Kansas City Southern's *Southern Belle* would sound, as it rolled into town. All the boys—at the age when hormones are in full gallop and proper decorum is an undervalued trait—would say in unison, "There she is! The beautiful 'Southern Belle.'" Then the crass ones would take turns, day after day, looking Alben's way to say, "But there's a-nother southern belle I'd like to ride."

Alben would blush but could not keep a slight smile off her face. She was blessed with good looks and knew it; but not in the way that made others hate her. In fact, she had a knack for being friendly to even an unpopular kid, boy or girl. Because, simply put, she was a friendly person. That, and her looks, was undoubtedly the reason she got elected homecoming queen her first year at Heavener High, the first freshman ever to do so.

She possessed what fashion and movie magazines describe as an hourglass figure: decidedly busty, tiny waist, and hips ample enough to be provocative—without being too ample!

"Mommy," a five-year-old Alben had complained one summer day after playing in the park, "Johnny Jenks called me 'bubble-butt!'"

"Well, what did you say?" Mrs. Barkley responded, stifling a laugh.

"I said, 'I do not!' Then I slapped him. "

"Now, Alben! It wasn't nice to hit him. If he ever says it again, just tell Johnny that probably means you'll grow up to have a beautiful hourglass figure."

"What's that?"

Then followed, the obligatory 'show and tell' as her mother called attention to the little hourglass egg-timer filled with salt, that stood on the kitchen cabinet. She pointed out the tiny 'waistline.' Thereafter, Alben kept hoping Johnny Jenks would call her bubble-butt again. He never did. And little Alben was disappointed.

###

Mrs. Barkley was right. There was no music anywhere on the Ford's radio dial. Every station Alben found was going with network coverage of the Truman-Barkley inaugural. Her shiny gold wristwatch with the thin black cord band, said it was seven minutes to eleven in Heavener. That should mean Uncle Alben would be sworn in shortly, and she could get on with her day; a day which needed to be meticulously timed.

Alben had the radio volume low as the news coverage droned on. She wanted to truthfully tell her mother she heard dear old Uncle Alben take the oath; but was not interested in minute details of the event. She had a few minutes to spare and wheeled into the Phillips 66 gas station, hopped out of the Ford, and went in.

"Hi, Delbert," she called to the fifteen-year-old kid at the cash register, "fill up the Ford. And give me a Coca-Cola. An icy, icy cold one." Alben knew he had a crush on her; and knew it made him feel good if she flirted with him.

Shy Delbert merely nodded, smiled, and blushed as he turned to the soda pop cooler and rummaged through the icy water. While he did this, Alben quickly unbuttoned the red coat so Delbert could see the short, plaid skirt. "Here," Delbert mumbled. "This one's real cold." He handed her the bottle, but his eyes were on Alben's bare knees.

"How much?" Alben asked, "I can't keep track of what they cost," she lied.

"Eight cents. We give ya three cents when ya bring the bottle back."

"Keep the change," Alben smiled as she slid a dime and a nickel all the way to the cash register, touching Delbert's hand in the process. She gave him a wink and returned to the Ford. Until Uncle Alben was sworn in, she would sit right here and drink her Coke. There were two other gas pumps, and she was at the one right next to the service station doorway. She knew Delbert would pass as close to the Ford as possible, every time he came out to pump someone's gas. Therefore, she tugged the plaid skirt three inches higher. That too, she thought, would make Delbert feel good.

Moments later—

Alben decided she best buy the train ticket now. She wanted that taken care of. She parked the Ford in a little nook she had scoped out days ago behind the depot; a small freight platform that was seldom used anymore. There was most always a spare boxcar parked between the spot and the street. The Ford was, for the most part, completely hidden. She pulled sunglasses from her purse, put them on, and turned her coat collar up. Alben then reached back in her purse and took out a gold-colored band. She had bought it in the toy department of Woolworth's, but it was shiny and looked real. She placed it on the fourth finger of her left hand. It would make the ticket agent less suspicious, she thought. She walked in the back door of the depot. Good! Only three people were sitting on the benches—she didn't recognize any of them—and the new ticket agent was alone behind the window.

"One-way to New Orleans, on this evening's *Southern Belle*," Alben said as casually as possible. "Coach."

The agent looked up, seemed a bit curious, but "Guess the sun's a little bright out there," is all he said.

"Yes. Yes it is." Alben could feel her heart pounding.

"There you are. That'll be $19.67. It leaves at 5:15—and it's most always on time."

Alben slid two tens under the window and the agent slid back the change. "Thank you, sir," and she was out the back door with the precious ticket—and off to the IGA grocery.

CHAPTER THREE
Tension...

3:51 p.m. —

Alben is sure her mother, standing at the kitchen stove, has to hear the pounding of her daughter's heart. Alben is also sure her strong pulse is moving the slightly visible lace trim of the foundation brassiere she recently bought at Montgomery Ward's. Then—she realizes the sound she's really hearing is the ticking of the grandfather clock, which has ticked every day of her life in the Barkley living room.

"Here, Alben dear, sit down"—Mrs. Barkley is at her motherly best— "you're so fidgety! Don't want you to ruin your supper, but bet you didn't eat any lunch. Or breakfast for that matter." Mrs. Barkley set a small plate on the table: a steaming half-sandwich of just-out-of-the-oven meat loaf. "I know it's your favorite. We won't tell your father. He wants you to keep that lovely figure. Just because he's the president of the Heavener branch of the Oklahoma State Bank—doesn't mean a cheerleading scholarship at Norman wouldn't be welcome." Mrs. Barkley smiled and patted the corner chair next to her at the kitchen table. "Sit, dear." And she took yet another sip, from yet another cup, of freshly brewed coffee. "So glad you heard Uncle Alben take the oath today. Wasn't it thrilling?"

"Yes, Momma." Alben wanted to wolf down the sandwich. Her tummy had been so full of butterflies all afternoon, she hadn't realized how starved she was. However, she was having trouble swallowing; not because of hunger, not because of nervousness. But because it might be a very long time, before her feet were under her parents' kitchen table again. If ever! Her eyes brimmed with hot salty tears. Would her mother see? One side of her brain screamed, Why? Why am I doing this stupid thing? But the other side screamed back, I…have…to!!

"Oh, Good Lord!" Mrs. Barkley was up in a flash and off to the stove. Fortunately, for Alben in her emotional moment, Momma had left the burner on under the coffee pot—and the enameled utensil was steaming, spluttering, and rocking like it was about to take flight.

For Alben, it was enough to break the nostalgic spell. She forced herself to think not of her mother, still muttering and wiping up spewed coffee from the stove; not to think of her dear father still at the bank, whom she would not see again until God only knew when; but to think of Joey, and how he felt when he pressed hard against her under the bleachers at the baseball park last summer, his lips against hers. How very much she wanted him! All of him!

If those romantic fantasies of her movie-infatuated youth were not enough to bring her mental state back where their escapade demanded, the next instant did. She glanced at her left hand on the table and saw what apparently—thankfully—her mother had not. Alben had forgotten to remove Woolworth's shiny gold band from the fourth finger of her left hand!

4:37 p.m.

The knots in Alben's stomach were about to explode. Her mother left religiously at 4:30 each Thursday afternoon, for her five o'clock appointment at the beauty parlor. She liked to get there early to catch up on the town gossip. She would never admit to that, but that's why she went early. However, Mrs. Barkley was running late today. She always took Fred the Dog with her. The pup would curl up on the front seat of the car and sleep till the hair appointment was over. All that was why a Thursday was chosen for the launch of the great escapade. No Momma Barkley around to ask questions; no Fred the Dog to bark, whimper, or whine if something seemed strange.

Finally, Alben heard the throaty purr of the Ford V-8 as the engine started up in the driveway. A sense of relief swept over her as the crunch of gravel under its whitewall tires became less discernible, meaning the automobile was moving down the street away from the house.

Alben was packed and ready to go. That she was traveling so light was a concern. Joey had warned that winter, even in New Orleans, could be very cold. But there was no reasonable alternative. She had packed only the medium-size black suitcase her mother seldom used. A bigger case would be too cumbersome for her to carry—but she would not leave her new red coat behind. However, she would not wear it now. The vibrant color would attract too much attention at dusk. Too many friends and acquaintances had seen her wear it. So the suitcase held the red coat, a pair of jeans, the eighth grade 'too short' plaid skirt—two blouses, one dressy dress, two pair of anklets, a pair of hose with seams, and three changes of underwear. She also took the black sweater her Aunt Sarah had given her a year ago.

"You'll get more good out of this now than I will," Sarah winked. Sarah had recently married. She had returned from her duties as a WAC in France, in late '45. She told Alben she bought the sweater at a little Paris boutique. It was very avant garde: thin cashmere, a scooped out neckline, and form-fitting to the max.

Alben also tucked her black and white saddle shoes in the inside pocket of the suitcase lid, and one more pair of hose with seams. And, folded as neatly as possible between her red coat and the dress, was a new filmy nightgown; not too short, not too long, but quite thin. Sheer, really. This was just in case. In case Joey asked her to marry him.

For the trip, she was wearing her new, smart-looking cape. She had made it in Home Ec, from a Vogue pattern, and had proven an excellent seamstress. The teacher gave Alben an A+. A silk blouse and the pearls she got for her sixteenth birthday made the classy outfit, more classy. The cape was of high quality black wool. She also wore black pumps with slender, gold heels; the same shoes she wore that time she talked to Joey at the soda fountain.

She had been saving her allowance, and ten days ago bought some classy material from the only dressmaker in town. The material was brilliant red. She again turned seamstress. For three nights, after her parents were in bed, she turned the red material into a short, tight skirt. Even shorter than her eighth grade plaid. Big slit up the right leg—a little longer in the back. She knew Joey would like that, even though it was now, somewhat unfashionable. But probably not in New Orleans, she thought. Alben also packed her other pair of hose with seams and the red tam.

She had tiptoed into her mother's bedroom, debated with her conscience, and decided Mrs. Barkley would not mind. She "borrowed" Momma's stunning silk scarf to wear around her neck. It was cold in Oklahoma in January, but since the depot was only a block-and-a-half away—with the scarf—she would be fine. She had just walked from her mother's bedroom when one more thought hit her: a hat! If she saw someone she knew; someone she did not want to see; a hat would help cover her face. She pulled a black one from her mother's top shelf. It fit perfectly.

She refused to reflect when she left the house. She pushed from her mind that it was the only home she'd ever known. She forced herself to think of Joey. She imagined him pressing hard against her. She loved him. She knew she did! She wanted to be with him. Why else would she do this? Some kids had mean parents. She didn't. Mister and Mrs. Barkley were good and kind to her. Was it just that she had read Ava Gardner was the rebellious type? Alben had nothing to rebel about. But she wanted to rebel. And By Jove! she was going to.

Alben was still a half-block from the depot when she first heard the distant airhorns of the *Southern Belle*. That meant the streamliner was crossing a farm-to-market road, about a mile north of Heavener. She quickened her pace.

In January, at five o'clock in Heavener, Oklahoma, the sun is not far from setting. It's dusk, to say the least. But Alben entered the depot cautiously, anyway. She was out of breath from carrying the suitcase.

The alcove at the back door had no light of its own. It was in the shadows. She peeked into the waiting room. Four people were just rising from the wooden benches, and moving toward the door to the loading platform. Did she know anyone? No. Good. WAIT!! Yes!!! One was Mister Scribner, who ran the soda fountain. Alben had seen him—and he, her— every day of her life since she was twelve.

She lingered in the shadows while reaching in her purse. Though the sun was almost down, she brought the sunglasses for just such an occasion. In reality, Alben would have worn the glasses if no one were in the depot. It was too good a scene, right out of any Hollywood film noir:

…catching a train at sundown… hoping no one would recognize her… would Ava Gardner wear sunglasses? …is the Pope Catholic??!!

Alben lingered in the alcove till the last moment. Then, she walked swiftly across the depot waiting room, the ricocheting sound of her high heels bouncing from the walls. She must see Mister Scribner at the top of the train steps. Would he take a coach to the right, or to the left? She would go in the opposite direction, and hope to high heaven they never once met in the aisle of any swaying coach!

CHAPTER FOUR
Exhilaration!

5:27 p.m.

She did it! She had not chickened out. Alben James Barkley—grand-niece of the Vice President of the United States of America—was running away to meet her boyfriend in New Orleans! Really, her fiancée. She must start thinking of him that way. That's what Joey was. Surely, that's what he was. For encouragement, she reached again in her purse, and pulled out Woolworth's gold band, placing it on the fourth finger of her left hand. She had once heard that was a good plan for attractive young ladies who travel. A ring was not a guarantee—but it just might keep an unwanted suitor at bay on a train.

Alben leaned her face against the cool window of the *Southern Belle*, as it picked up speed. The pane was mostly frosted over, from the contrast of heat inside, cold outside. She touched her lips to the soothing glass, admired the imprint of perfect lips she left there; then did it again. But this time she was not kissing a streamliner window pane. This time she was kissing Joey. And in her innermost being, she felt his strong body against her.

It was difficult for Alben to remember precisely, the first time the idea of running away had been born. Had it started as mere fantasy? a wild idea? a thrilling, sensual imagining they had no serious thought of carrying out? Probably. She did recall the conversation that occurred at Scribner's four days after their first meeting. It was the day after Alben had been dressed up for the Home Ec project.

Joey was sipping on his cherry coke through a straw, looking at her sideways out the corner of his eye. He'd been talking of how he dreaded the end of his two-week leave; then, he got a silly little grin on his face.

"What? What?" Alben asked, perplexed and a little embarrassed by this closeup scrutiny.

"You look a lot younger than you did yesterday," Joey replied.

"What do you mean?"

"Oh… you're wearin' blue jeans and saddle shoes today. Yesterday—in that tight skirt and high heels, you looked about thirty-three."

Alben blushed.

"Sittin' there, danglin' that high heel all over creation…" Joey thoroughly enjoyed the memory—and enjoyed recounting it to Alben, knowing it embarrassed and pleased her all at the same time. "That's mighty distractin' to a sailor boy like me," he chuckled.

"Well, maybe we should just run away and meet in some seaport." Alben could not believe she had just said that! Her face had to be absolutely crimson. "I'm being silly," she whispered sheepishly.

"Well, maybe not," was Joey's quiet response. "I could get another leave the last half of January. And if I had a good reason—I just might."

And somewhere out of that conversation, the entire scheme had been hatched. They worked out details the last day Joey was in town. He borrowed his aunt's late model panel truck—a Chevy, two-tone green—washed and waxed it, then picked up Alben at 4:30 in the afternoon. With her showing him the way, they drove the nine miles to Lake Wister, nestled in small mountains which were covered with pine and oak. The lake was created by the waters of the Poteau and Fourche Maline Rivers. The young would-be lovers sat on the shore until well after sunset, then sat for another hour in the truck necking, in much more intimate fashion than Alben would ever tell anyone.

By the time they headed back to Heavener the details were worked out between them: Alben's slipping out of town aboard the *Southern Belle*, Joey taking the January leave, and flying down to New Orleans to find accommodations. He said a Navy C-47—the "Gooney Bird" they called it—made a run once or twice a month out of Portsmouth to the Big Easy, carrying some sort of cargo. What the hell it was, he had no idea—but Joey knew one of the pilots. The pilot had told him anytime he wanted to hitch a ride home, just let him know.

Joey had written Alben on New Year's Day, to say his pilot buddy was scheduled out at 0800 hours, Thursday, January 20—and "I'll meet my southern belle on the *Southern Belle* the morning of the 21st—New Orleans—Kansas City Southern station. I can't wait! Be on the damn train!"

Alben didn't think she actually lied to her mother about that day at the lake; but did recall the impression was left—one way or another—that she had gone to Lake Wister with a bunch of kids. Joey Thibodeaux was not mentioned.

What Alben was to do at the end of the ten or eleven days in New Orleans had not really been discussed. And she refused to dwell on it. She had been faithful in what they had pledged to each other: to save up as much money as possible, so they could have fun in the city where fun was the primary pursuit. She had cut her spending at Scribner's Soda Shop in half, and had baby-sat more often than she really wanted. So now—except for the purchase of the nightgown, fancy undies, etc. —and the train ticket—the stash was in tact. As she left Heavener, she had $101 in that secret slot, beneath the fake silk lining of her purse. Plus the twenty-dollar bill and a little change, in the tiny snap coin section. That was for food, or whatever, on the *Southern Belle* ride to New Orleans.

CHAPTER FIVE
Alone... And Afraid

8:35 p.m.

The *Southern Belle* rolled to a stop in Texarkana right on time. A traveling salesman was sitting in the seat directly across the aisle from Alben, talking to a fellow salesman. "Ya know, they tell me that when the *Southern Belle* stops at this depot, one end of the train is in Arkansas—the other in Texas. "

"Which end ya think we're (burp) sittin' in?" his buddy asked, nursing a half-hidden bottle in a paper bag. "I sure hope it's the pretty end." The over-served fellow began giggling; that silly giggle that so often accompanies too much alcohol. In seconds, both salesmen were laughing in a ridiculous manner, though nothing was really fuuny. But it was infectious. In seconds, everyone in the coach—including Alben—was laughing like Jack Benny had just told a joke. However, the laughter died as fast as it started, because there was nothing all that humorous except the gentlemen's ridiculous conversation.

The porter had walked through the cars just moments ago, informing passengers that the city on the Arkansas-Texas border was a twenty-five minute stop tonight. Why, he didn't say. But the porter went on to say they were all welcome to get off and stretch their legs, if they so desired. "Just make sure, ya gotch yer ticket stub to get back on," he added.

Alben decided a little walk was a good idea. In case everyone else got off, she certainly did not want to be left alone with the drunk salesmen.

The Texarkana depot was warm and bright. The sizzling sound and aroma of frying hamburgers emanated from the lunch counter. It struck Alben that she was starved—but she wanted to eat in the *Southern Belle* dining car. The porter had announced earlier that the final dinner seating in the dining car, would be immediately upon their departure from Texarkana. That sounded perfect to Alben.

She wandered to the magazine stand and bought the latest edition of *Vogue*. She had developed an intense interest in style and fashion; not all that surprising, considering her addiction to Hollywood and the silver screen. Her eyes then glanced over the newspaper rack. There, peering at her from this morning's Texarkana Gazette, were separate formal photographs of Harry Truman and Uncle Alben Barkley. The pictures were accompanied by the story of their pending inauguration at mid-day. But it was the second headline above the fold of the Gazette—off to the side— that made Alben freeze:

TWO SAILORS DEAD IN EXPLOSION

PORTSMOUTH NAVAL SHIPYARD

The sub-headline was worse. It made her blood run cold:

ONE FROM CONWAY, ARKANSAS;

THE OTHER FROM LOUISIANA

Alben almost threw the money for the magazine and paper at the clerk and ran to the train. Gasping for breath, shaking, her heart in her throat, she sat down in her coach seat and switched on the reading light. She quickly read the short paragraph of the story, but was scarcely enlightened further. It had happened just last evening: a spark of electricity—that's what they surmised—had ignited a huge gasoline tank. Nothing else. No names. No other details.

Alben stared out the window, a horrible paralyzing fear gripping her as she heard the "All a-boARRRRD!" from the conductor, hanging from the coach steps. The *Southern Belle* began its slow roll. What if Joey were dead? What if he were the Louisiana sailor in the story? Why had she agreed to this crazy, childish adventure? She wished she could jump from the train and walk back home. But that was an even more childish thought. Utterly silly.

Alben felt totally drained. Her adrenalin-charged day was catching up with her. She completely forgot her hunger pangs and turned her face to the frosty window, staring into the passing darkness. Huge tears began to roll down her cheeks. She had never been so scared in her life. She was too immobilized to do anything; all thought gone of a fancy dinner in the dining car. Totally exhausted… she drifted into slumber.

Alben awoke with a start. The *Southern Belle* was highballing through the night. It seemed to be going faster than at anytime during the trip. Alben's throat was parched and dry from the coach's heating system—and she had to pee! Now!

She closed the door of the tiny washroom behind her, making sure to lock it securely. It was not all that comfortable, rocking back and forth on a commode—at eighty miles an hour.

Alben was shocked when she looked in the dingy mirror over the tiny metal wash basin. Her eyes were puffy and red from crying herself to sleep. The warm water felt good as she washed out her eyes again and again; then, continued the cleansing with the same amount of cold water. All this meant redoing her makeup.

She finally emerged from the washroom fifteen minutes later, none the worse for wear, except for the haunting fear that still gripped her. She re-entered the coach, squinting to find the seat she'd been sitting in. She paused. That's when she felt the man's hand on her rump.

"Helllll-LOOOO, pretty lady!" Yet another over-served gentlemen. This one was making no attempt to hide the paper bag, or the bottle he was sipping from.

Alben was quick to retort. "Keep your hands to yourself, please!" She found her seat and resumed staring into the darkness. She tried to tell herself she was foolish to be so afraid. There were undoubtedly many—hundreds if not thousands, of young patriotic sailors in the United States Navy from Louisiana; many even stationed at Portsmouth. But deep down her worst fears continued to nag.

Sometime later: the conductor hurried past her down the aisle, mumbling, "…damn it! We're runnin' late!" Those were the only words Alben heard…before she again fell asleep.

10:20 p.m.

It was the screech of steel against steel that awakened her. The *Southern Belle* was braking, slowing abruptly. Alben's coach stopped directly in front of a small depot. She spotted the marquee just as the porter called, "Rooo-dess-uh, Luuuzzzz-an-UH!" Rodessa. Joey's hometown! Alben's heart was again in her throat. What if Joey's body was already en route home? To right here! This town!

What happened next did not help. She heard the sound of metal wheels rolling slowly on the cement of the loading platform, before the wooden luggage cart came into view alongside her window. It was being pulled by an elderly Negro man. Only one item was on the cart: a ghostly, silver grey casket!

No! It's not possbile. She grabbed the Texarkana newspaper to make certain she had read the story correctly. Yes. She had. The Portsmouth explosion had occurred just last evening. It was utterly inconceivable the body of that poor Louisiana sailor—whoever it might be—could just now be taken off the *Southern Belle* in Rodessa. There just wasn't time. The knowledge of the time frame began to slow her rapidly beating heart and she began to relax a little. But in the back of her mind, it still nagged. Could the same Navy flight which Joey was to ride to New Orleans?…Could that same flight instead, have dropped his casket in Texarkana; where it was then loaded aboard the *Southern Belle?* Was that why the *Southern Belle* was running late? Why there was a longer stop than usual in Texarkana? Had that taken the extra time?

This is crazy, she told herself. She must calm down. She was so tired, wanting desperately to sleep; to awaken to golden sunshine; and Joey! In New Orleans. For a split second she was tempted to ask one of the whiskey-sipping men in the coach for a swig. Maybe that would help her sleep. But she did not have the guts to ask a stranger for a drink, especially from the same bottle he'd been sipping. She moved closer to the window, laid her forehead against the cool glass, and softly cried until she again fell asleep.

Friday, January 21, 1949
6:43 a.m.

Alben wasn't sure what awakened her. Was it the grey light of morning infusing the *Southern Belle* coach? Was it the high speed of the streamliner making sure it arrived in the 'Big Easy' on time? The train was rocking like a baby's crib, at the hand of a loving mother. Or was it just that Alben's face had slid down to the very bottom of the frosty window pane, her bottom lip crammed till it hurt, against the metal frame below the pane? She quickly grabbed her compact mirror from her purse, and stared with horror at her face. Mascara, rouge! Everything was streaked in grotesque lines across her Ava Gardner face.

"What time is it?" It was almost a yell, at the unsuspecting passing porter.

Startled, he turned to Alben, his eyes wide. "Uh—it's… uh… it's twenty to s-seven," he stammered.

"Sorry." She was embarrassed at her jumpiness. "What—what time are we due in New Orleans?"

"Seven-thirty," he replied, "but we're running about twenty-five minutes behind."

Good! Alben had an hour, to an hour-and-a-half. Grabbing her suitcase from the overhead rack, she rushed past the porter, praying the washroom was empty. It was. Which was wonderful. She had to pee again!

CHAPTER SIX
Panic!

8:12 a.m.

Finally, Alben was together. She had spent too much time redoing her makeup; so she quickly chose an outfit: the too short red skirt she was wearing, and Aunt Sarah's tight black sweater. Yes! She pulled a pair of seamed hose from her suitcase. No, she thought, New Orleans can't be that cold. She pulled her saddle shoes from the case, sat down on the commode to put them on and—NO! Alben was now a grown up girl. A young lady. She would keep wearing the black pumps with gold heels—her legs bare! But just in case Joey had been right, and New Orleans was a cold city today, she pulled her new red winter coat from the case, and put it on.

And one last touch to her hair: she pulled from the bottom of her purse one other item purchased with money from her stash. She got it at Smith's Jewelry in Heavener. It was a tiny jeweled hair barrette, gold-colored with diamonds—fake, of course. But it was pretty. And on sale: $6.95, marked down from $15.95. She had to wear this! Alben had seen Ava Gardner wear such a barrette in at least two publicity photos. She placed it in her thick chestnut hair near her right ear, pushing her hair forward on that side, almost to her eye.

Alben got back to her seat a mere three minutes before the *Southern Belle* rolled to a stop at the Kansas City Southern station. She had been so busy getting ready to meet Joey, the horrifying fear of the night before was pushed to the back of her mind. But now, it again seeped into her consciousness.

"Newwww Orrrr-lee-uhns," the porter called. "Home ag'in, home ag'in, jiggety-jig," he laughed.

Alben was the last one to leave her seat, walking tentatively to the vestibule and the coach steps. As her feet touched the concrete loading platform in New Orleans, Louisiana, she instantly knew Joey was wrong about one thing. The temperature had to be seventy degrees, at least; not a trace of Joey's warning of an often damp and frigid January in New Orleans. Not on this morning. She immediately set her suitcase down, shucked out of her red winter coat, and laid it across the case.

Alben turned to her right; to her left. No Joey. The paralyzing fear increased, slowly at first, then with each passing second it swelled in intensity. She was short of breath, and franticly began to walk; one direction, then the other. Oh, God! Please, dear God! No! I can't breathe. He can't be dead! No, dear God, please!! Tears began to pour down her cheeks. Joey! Where are you, Joey?

At that moment a long black car—a Fleetwood Cadillac—slowly rounded the corner and pulled to a stop just yards from Alben. A woman in a beautiful fur coat alighted from the limousine. The coat was sliver fox, Alben thought. The lady was dainty, with a hauntingly beautiful face. She looked familiar to Alben. But she could not quite place her.

"Honey…"—the woman had a concerned look on her face, as she gazed at Alben—"Honey, are you alright? You look… I'm sorry, you look terrified."

"No… no,"—Alben tried to be brave—just annoyed. My boyfrie—uh, husband," she mumbled, casually patting her hair so the Woolworth ring was visible, "he's… he's late. "

"Don't worry, dear." The woman smiled. "Men! They're always late. When you actually want to see them."

"Miss Miles!" The lady's driver was insistent. "Ma'm, we must go. You'll miss your train." The man was carrying two suitcases, and the porter had already loaded a baggage car with enough luggage for a six-week sea voyage.

"I'm sure he'll be here shortly," the woman smiled at Alben, and she was gone.

Alben muttered a "thank you," but turned quickly away before the lady could see more tears of horror, which were about to stream from her eyes. She started to run; to run in the opposite direction. Anywere. But knew not where to go. "Oh, dear GOD!" she pleaded.

Behind her, she heard the sound of a roaring engine, and screeching tires. A '48 Chrysler—a bright yellow one—rounded the corner. A Yellow Cab. It stopped right in front of Alben's suitcase and coat. The rear door of the Chrysler swung open …and out stepped Petty Officer 3rd Class Joey J. Thibodeaux, United States Navy, of Rodessa, Louisiana. His smile was wide—his open arms wider.

Alben could not recall running the few yards to Joey. She could only assume she flew. She jumped into his arms, her bare legs encircling his waist as he ever so slowly began to turn around in a tight circle. And around, and around. To Alben, it seemed it was slow-motion eternity, filled with flashback memories of being with Joey beneath the Heavener stadium bleachers. And in the panel truck at Lake Wister. For a brief second she thought of shy Delbert at the Phillips 66—and wondered what he would think if he saw her right now. Would he be happy for her? sad? jealous? Or would he just think she was cheap? No time to linger on such thoughts. Alben was in Joey's arms. This... is heaven! Her lips smothered his face, his hair, his neck, his sailor cap, and—his lips. And Joey's body was pressed against her.

Alben James Barkley—age sixteen and-a-half—in Joey Thibodeaux's arms! In the Big Easy!

CHAPTER SEVEN
Fancy Eggs

"**W**hat??!!" The explosive response came from Joey immediately after asking Alben, if she ate breakfast on the *Southern Belle*. That was the first time she remembered—which she relayed to Joey—that she had not had a single bite since her mother's meat loaf sandwich yesterday afternoon.

"Owen Brennan's place," Joey said as he tapped the cabbie on the shoulder. "It's on Bourbon Street."

"I know, I know," said the cabbie.

"Is it true he'll fix a fancy breakfast for a few people?" Joey asked, then added, "If you sneak in the side door?"

"Depends on whether I get outa the car and knock on the side door," the driver smiled. "Owen always takes my fares, anytime I bring 'em."

"Vera Miles!" Alben suddenly shouted.

Joey looked at her like she was insane. "Who?"

"Vera Miles," Alben smiled, "a new Hollywood actress. I just met her at the train station. Couldn't remember her name. But she's real nice."

"Never heard of her," Joey responded.

"Like I said. She's new. I saw her in a movie a month or so ago. *Two Tickets To Broadway*, I think it was. She was born in Oklahoma; and was once Miss Kansas."

"Whoop-dee-do," Joey teased.

Alben gave him a light punch in the tummy. "Smarty!" she said. "I bet she was here to promote that movie—or a new one. "She grabbed his arm, and snuggled as close as she could. Contented now, she gazed out the taxi window at the buildings of New Orleans; a place she'd always heard of, but never seen. What an adventure! She laid her head on her sailor boy's shoulder. *I wonder if Vera Miles thought I looked like Ava Gardner.*

They were led to a small table in a tiny alcove. It was as though Mister Brennan recognized two young people who would appreciate a little privacy. But they could still see out onto Bourbon Street.

"You like eggs benedict?" Joey asked.

"What's that?"

"Uh, poached eggs—you like poached eggs?"

"They're okay," Alben responded slowly. "Momma fixes 'em for me when I've been sick. "

Joey laughed and added, "Eggs benedict in N'orluhns are more than just poached eggs. And people eat 'em when they ain't sick. Comes with a little ham–er, I think they call it Canadian bacon—and maybe some fancy spinach on a buttered English muffin. Then, they pour hollandaise sauce all over it."

"What's that?" Alben asked. She didn't remember that from Home Ec.

"It's, uh… oh hell! I don't know. But it's good. How do you like your eggs?"

"A little runny—but not too much."

Joey ordered their eggs benedict medium, with cheese grits, "… and two Bloody Marys."

Alben raised her eyebrows as the waiter moved away.

"Oh, I didn't think," he apologized, "have you ever had a drink?"

"You got to be kidding!" Alben retorted. "Under the football stadium in Heavener? Don't tell me you forgot!"

"Oh, right," Joey smiled. "My hip flask. Mister Jim Beam, as I recall."

"I don't know what it was," Alben giggled. "Tasted horrible. I just meant—what's the drinking age here?"

"Uh, eighteen, I think. But relax. You look very grownup. And they just don't ask a lotta questions in N'orluhns."

Alben did relax. "No matter the taste, I must admit: the stuff in your flask made me feel good. "

"So does a Bloody Mary," Joey replied.

And 'twas so. Particularly after each had two. And not a crumb was left of Owen Brennan's fancy eggs, or anything else.

CHAPTER EIGHT
Bargain Rate

"We're real close," Joey said. "214 Royal Street. "They had walked only five minutes from Brennan's location on Bourbon. Joey was toting Alben's suitcase. "There it is. Half-block ahead," he said. Then he stopped. "Uh… here's the deal. Don't ever go to the front desk. No need to," Joey added as he took two keys from his pocket and handed one to Alben.

"Whaddya mean?"Alben was perplexed.

"It's taken care of." Joey smiled. "The concierge at the Hotel Monteleone—his kid brother is stationed with me at Portsmouth. Poker buddy. He owes me. A lot. This is his way of payin' off."

Alben was breathless as they walked into the opulent lobby. "I've never seen anything like this," she whispered, staring at the huge chandelier. "Won't somebody get wise and kick us out?"

"Nope." Joey smiled and nodded to the man at the concierge desk, took Alben by the hand, and led her directly to the elevator. "The man I just nodded to; that's my buddy's brother. He got the register at the front desk, and entered Room 310 as 'blocked' for redecoration. He'll keep it that way till we leave." The elevator door closed behind them. "Three, please," he said to the operator; then in a whisper to Alben, "They ain't quite so busy in January."

The thick carpet in the long hallway to 310 seemed to envelope the soles and heels of Alben's pumps. And when Joey opened the door for her—well! If she were surprised at the glamour of the hotel itself, she was doubly so by the room. In the first place, it was triple the size of her comfy bedroom in Heavener. An elegant chest of drawers with mirror was against the wall to the left. The room was not gilded; not even ostentatious. It was just so tasteful—and rich looking.

And to the right—the bed! It was what Alben had feared, but hoped against. It was one bed. She had hoped for—what had she hoped for? Twin beds? There was not even a couch in the room long enough to sleep on. Instead, there were three comfortable easy chairs, an antique-looking table alongside each, and a decorative reading lamp on each table.

Joey saw the discomfort on Alben's face and knew immediately the problem. "Oh, look honey. Don't worry. I'm in the Navy. I can sleep anywhere. I'll use the extra pillow and blanket in the closet and sleep on the floor. It'll all be fine."

Alben smiled in relief and hugged him, but down deep feared such resolve would quickly wane. For both.

"Come on. Let's go. I wanna show you my big city!" Joey was intent upon changing the subject as quickly as possible. He wanted to take Alben's mind away from the one bed. Alben dashed into the bathroom to change into jeans and her saddle shoes, Joey proudly sticking to his Navy blues and white sailor cap. With luggage safely in their room, and the room keys safely in Joey's pocket, this time they strolled leisurely through the gilded Monteleone lobby.

"What's everbody lookin' at?" Alben asked. She pointed to a small crowd, standing clustered together, their backs to three, large leather couches; the settees arranged in the shape of a 'u'. "Why ain't they settin' down?"

"Oh!" Joey exclaimed. "I'll bet it's that new picture-box thing."

"What?"

"Television," Joey explained. "New Orleans got a television station last month."

Alben had heard of television. She read about it in movie magazines. But knew no one in Heavener owned one. Why should they? There were no television stations they could pick up. Alben remembered reading once in the "Weekly Reader" at school, that some guy over in Springfield, Missouri, had one of those little picture boxes. And that he occasionally picked up a blurry signal from an experimental station in Kansas City. A television school had set up business in that town back in the '30s. But not much had come of it in her part of the country.

Joey grabbed her hand and pushed into the crowd—mostly men—who politely parted when they saw the pretty young girl. Then, Alben heard something familiar: "I, Alben William Barkley, do solemnly swear…"

"Joey!" she said. "That's him!"At that moment the last tall gentleman in front of her stepped aside, and there on a brilliant glass tube in the middle of a wooden cabinet, was the image of a rather rotund man with white wavy hair. He held his right hand aloft, and faced a black-robed judge. A woman stood between them, and appeared to be holding an open Bible. Alben recognized the rotund man from the picture on the Heavener living room wall. "Joey, that's Uncle Alben! This must be a newsreel. I heard that on the radio yesterday."

"Yes," said the tall man who had stepped aside for her. "Fox Movietone.

WSDU had it flown in overnight. Louisiana's first television station! Just went on the air last month. We're mighty proud of that here in N'orluhns."

And at this moment, the much younger Alben Barkley from Heavener, Oklahoma; the girl with the middle name of James; after all the years she's heard ad nauseam about her famous great-uncle, she finally felt a tingly surge of pride from the tip of her painted toenails, to the crown of her wavy chestnut hair. Her great-uncle, whom she's never met, and never will, is Vice-President of the United States of America! And he's in a Movietone newsreel—and better yet—on television! Wow!

4:10 p.m.

"I've never seen such a big river," Alben said dreamily.

"Course you haven't," Joey teased, "you're from land-locked Oklahoma."

To Alben, the mighty Mississippi looked a mile wide at the Port of New Orleans. It was not, but it looked that way. Joey and Alben had lingered in the Monteleone lobby a few additional moments to see President Truman take the oath of office, and then set off on a leisurely stroll through the old city. They visited Jackson Square and The Cathedral-Basilica of Saint Louis, King of France—the oldest Catholic cathedral in continuous use in the United States. It was her first visit to a Catholic cathedral and she was awed at the elaborate, old world handiwork and decor.

And they stopped in a half-dozen dixieland jazz bars on their trek, downing a beer here and there. As the afternoon wore on, an occasional cloud would block the sun, and the temperature dropped. They ducked into a dime store, and Alben picked up a pullover sweater in blue. It matched her eyes perfectly.

Now at the riverfront, "What is this?" Joey grabbed Alben's hand and pulled her twenty yards down the wharf. The eye-catching boat tied at a small dock was a sparkling 17-foot Chris Craft Deluxe Runabout. It sported golden brown varnished wood, with brown leather seats—front and back—and a gleaming white ivory steering wheel at the right side pilot's position. The boat's name was in gold letters on the stern. *Love On The River* it said.

"Wow!" Joey exclaimed. "Wanna ride?" He'd just noticed the hand-lettered sign: "20-min. ride $5—45-min. $10."

"Sure!" Alben squealed.

Joey handed a ten-dollar bill to the young guy in khakis, navy-colored peacoat, and a St. Louis Browns baseball cap. "What if we're through in twenty minutes?" Joey asked.

"I'll give you your change back," the kid smiled, "but you"ll be fine. Get in the back seat. There's a locker right underneath—and you'll find a big wool blanket there. It'll more than keep ya warm."

The guy in the Browns cap keyed the KL engine, and it roared to life. He backed away from the dock in a perfectly executed U-turn, then shifted gears and eased the throttle full forward. The nose of the Chris Craft lifted, and the runabout plowed into the wide Mississippi leaving a five-foot picturesque spray of silver, mixed with red and gold as the sun darted in and out from behind the clouds. The perfect 'V' of the craft's wake seemed a continuous ongoing portrait, being painted by an inspired maritime artist. It reminded Alben of the painting on her mother's bedroom wall. She had gazed at it years ago; one of the first times she put her newly acquired—and slightly accelerated—reading skills to work. It had burned into her brain. It was titled *Romance of Sail*; the artist was Frank Vining Smith. She had to have her mother's help, when first pronouncing 'Romance' and 'Vining'.

Under the heavy wool blanket, Alben snuggled close to Joey, and he pulled her closer still. This, Alben thought, this! is everything I knew it would be.

CHAPTER NINE
Passage

8:21 p.m.

"Miss Barkley," Joey called from his easy chair in Room 310. "Your sailor boy is about to starve." He had already leafed through the sports pages of the *New Orleans Times-Picayune* twice.

Alben smiled at her reflection in the bathroom mirror, said nothing, but added a finishing touch to her mascara and lipstick. She opened the door and stepped out in the one dressy dress she brought with her.

"Wow!" That's all Joey said. Whispered, really. When they returned to their room following the boat ride, he had told her to dress up for tonight. "It's our first night in N'orluhns. This is a big night—we'll tighten up the budget from here on out."

And big it was for the lovebirds. Dinner at Antoine's, where Alben got up the nerve to tell Joey of the headline she saw in Texarkana; and the ensuing panic attack it caused.

"Forget it," Joey smiled, as he reached across the table to take both of her hands in his. "Blot it from your mind. I'm here, ain't I?"

"Yes you are!" she replied, brushing away the tear that rolled down her cheek.

Then off they went, to bar-hop the French Quarter. Two hours after leaving Antoine's, Alben could not recall how many jazz, blues, and dance halls they hit. But it wasn't far shy of a dozen.

As the happy and slightly inebriated couple walked back toward the Monteleone, Alben began to shiver. She had not worn a coat over her fancy dress. And the night had turned cold, a brisk north wind whipping through the Quarter.

"Cabbie!" Joey yelled, and the passing taxi stopped immediately. "Come on, baby. Get in," he said to Alben, "don't want you catchin' cold." He held her close on the short three-block ride to the hotel. He still had one arm tightly around her waist as he unlocked the door to 310.

They were not three steps into the room when Alben turned abruptly, threw her arms around Joey's neck, and kissed him longer, and more passionately, than she ever had. Even more than at Lake Wister. She finally pushed against Joey's chest and stepped away. She had to catch her breath. When she looked into his eyes, she was suddenly scared. She knew what she saw in his eyes. More importantly, she knew what she felt. "I… I," she stammered, "I need a bath."Alben ducked quickly into the bathroom and closed the door. She ran the tub as long and deep as she dared, making sure it would not run over, shucked out of her fancy dress and undies, and submerged up to her neck. She hoped the deep passions she was feeling would subside. Instead, they seemed to increase. She washed herself thoroughly with the luxurious soap and thick washrag provided by the Montelone; then finally crawled from the tub and toweled dry with the huge white towel. There was a night candle on the large lavatory basin. She lit it and turned out the electric light. The candle provided just as much light, but softer. She retouched her makeup, then pulled the sheer nightie from her suitcase. Should she? The question was superfluous. She knew she would, regardless of the fluttering butterflies in her tummy. She pulled the gauzy material over her head and looked in the mirror! Her involuntary quick intake of breath expressed how little the nightie covered. Nothing!

Nevertheless, Alben opened the bathroom door and stepped into the bedroom, quietly pulling the door closed behind her. Or so she thought.

The room was dark, except for the lights of the street through the half-open window curtains. Joey was lying on the floor, wrapped in the hotel's extra blanket, his back to her.

"Joey," she whispered. Perhaps he was already asleep. Five seconds passed; then he slowly turned to face her just as the bathroom door, from natural gravity, swung slowly open behind Alben. Candle light behind her; lights from Royal Street glowing in front of her. She knew she was standing naked before him, save for the barely-there, gauzy nightie.

"Joey... please," she said softly, "I don't want you sleeping on the floor. You stay on your side of the bed—I'll stay on mine." With that she quickly turned, blew out the bathroom candle, and jumped beneath the covers of the large bed. In the light from the street, she saw Joey walk slowly to the bed in his undershorts and lie down. He did not turn his back to her. So she turned hers to him. Sixty seconds later, she felt his fingers touch her back. He traced his fingernails in little circles over the sheer nightgown. He then began to stroke her long hair, softly, slowly. Then back to little circles on her back. A moment later, Joey's hands moved down to lightly caress Alben's hips through the thin nightie.

Alben doubted mightily, they would stick to their own side of the bed, throughout the long night. And they did not.

CHAPTER TEN
In The Cold Grey Light Of Morning

Saturday, January 22, 1949
7:47 a.m.

Something awakened Alben. What was it? Was it dawn streaming through the window? She was lying on her back, the covers at her waist, and instinctly reached to pull the sheet to her neck as her breasts were fully exposed through the nightie.

It was then she realized that Joey was not in the bed; not in the room, nor the bathroom. It must have been the sound of the door quietly closing behind him, that had awakened her. She jumped from the bed and ran to the window. She could make out Joey's Navy blues a block-and-a-half down Royal, walking away. Is he leaving me? No, she told herself. I'm done with stupid fear. He showed up, didn't he? Just like he said he would. She knew he loved her. He had told her so over and over, during the night's recurring lovemaking. She knew she loved him. But... she would feel better if he returned quickly.

She stuffed her long hair into the Monteleone shower cap; was barely able to get it all in; then stepped into a hot shower.

Toweling dry, she wrapped the towel around her and slid up the room's biggest window. She stuck her head and hand out to check the temperature. Still chilly.

Alben turned on the table model radio and began to dress. Her new pullover sweater and jeans would keep her plenty warm under her red winter coat.

The radio commercial for Luzianne coffee ended and the sounds of a steel guitar filled the room. Alben recognized the smooth lyric baritone immediately. George Morgan was a new singer out of Nashville, Tennessee. She liked him a lot, and thought "Candy Kisses" would be a big hit.

Joey had been gone now almost two hours. Alben was beginning to get a little nervous. She still sat on the bed barefooted, brushing her hair over and over. Then. Thank God!

Joey entered with two paper sacks. "Well! Sleepyhead is up," he teased.

"Whatcha got?" Alben asked.

"Café Du Monde and Beignets."

"What's that?"

"Don't worry. You'll like it. "

"Ain't never seen no square donuts," Alben said five minutes later; but was already on her third one, and sipped sparingly of the coffee. It seemed a little bitter, but was tolerable because the brew was about half milk. She rarely drank coffee anyway—just when she had goofed off, then needed to study all night.

"Alben—" Joey started the sentence in a tenative way—"I wanna talk about something.'

What's coming now? she wondered.

"Alben—" he started again—"are you Catholic?"

"No," she laughed, "I'm Church of Christ." She laughed again. "I'm from Oklahoma, Joey. Most everybody is Church of Christ or Baptist."

"Yeah. "Joey joined in the laughter. "I s'pose so. Sorta like Louisiana. Everbody here is either Catholic or Baptist. The Thibodeauxs? We're Cajun. And Catholic."

"Whacha gettin' at, Joey?"

"Sweetheart, I know last night was not exactly as… as you wanted it to be. I mean—it was wonderful—but I know you would've liked a ring… and a ceremony."

Alben said nothing. She munched on her beignet and looked at her bare feet.

"That… that was your first time… wasn't it?" he said.

"Yes." Alben still stared at her feet. She did not want to know whether it was Joey's first.

Joey reached in the pocket of his uniform and pulled out a tiny velvet casket. He got down on one knee in front of Alben, and opened the ring box to reveal a gold band, with a small marquis diamond. "I want to marry you Alben. Today! It's—it's not much, just from a pawn shop down the street. Guess we can't have a priest… but…"

Alben's lips trembled and she began to cry. "It's beautiful, Joey. But how? …What would we do? I'm only sixteen. Don't we need a license?"

"That can be arranged. That's why I was gone so long for the beignets."

"But I got another year-and-a-half of high school, Joey."

"They got schools in New Hampshire, Alben—and Maine. And I'm in my second hitch for Uncle Sam; which means I can live off base. We'll get us a cozy little apartment."

"With what? We don't have any money."

"Look. You might have to waitress a couple of hours after school before ya do homework. Just till I get out of the Navy. But we can do it, Alben." Joey was selling with everything he had. "I love you, Alben."

She smiled at him through her tears. "And I love you, Joey. "She grabbed his neck and kissed him deeply on the mouth. This may have started as a lark. But they'd gone too far to turn back. It was time to grow up. She would do the daring, rebellious thing—just as she was sure, Ava Gardner would! "Joey," she said through joyful tears, "I'll marry you. Let's get this show on the road!"

Joey's whoop of joy was probably heard through even the thick walls of the Monteleone. "Great!" he yelled. "Put your party dress on. The Justice of the Peace said he's in his office till noon today."

Alben jumped up and shucked out of her jeans and sweater. She didn't bother to hide in the bathroom now. In fact, she suddenly enjoyed walking around in front of Joey in her undies. And he seemed quite content to sit in an easy chair and watch, as she slipped a garter belt around her waist, then carefully pulled on a pair of seamed hose; making sure the seam was precisely straight—and in the center—of each leg. She then walked to the closet and put on her pumps. Only then, did she pull her dressy dress over her head, and cover her body. Somehow, she seemed to fill out the dress in more provocative fashion, than ever before.

11:25a.m.

Alben walked the five blocks to the Justice of the Peace, holding Joey's hand. "Did you… did you have to bribe him?" she asked.

"Of course not," Joey protested. "That's illegal. And I'm in the United States Navy. "

Alben looked up at Joey. Was he speaking 'tongue in cheek'? He appeared serious. "Does he know I'm only sixteen?"

"Yes. "

"Well, did… didn't he ask any questions?"

"Only one. "

"And?"

Joey seemed hesitant to answer… but did. "He asked if we… if we had been to bed… in the manner of married folk."

Alben remained silent.

"And I said, 'Yes,'" Joey concluded.

Alben wondered if she'd be able to look at the judge… is a Justice of the Peace a judge? She thought so …she wondered if she'd be able to look him in the eye.

CHAPTER ELEVEN
Mr. and Mrs.

11:50 a.m.

"Helllll-EHHHHHN??!!" The sudden eruption from the Honorable Justice of the Peace Lamont Dupré was so loud, Alben and Joey both jumped. "Sorry, little lady," the Justice smiled, "just callin' my secretary. She'll need to act as your witness."

The slightly plump, middle-aged secretary, entered the chamber quickly from a side door.

"You know the routine, Helen. You need to witness the procedures for these young people, then sign the documents." He paused, shuffling papers. "Now." The judge looked directly at Alben. "Young lady, do you have any kind of identification?"

"Yes, your honor. "Alben reached in her purse. She was glad Joey had reminded her to say 'Your Honor' every time she addressed Mister Dupré. She handed him her Oklahoma driver's license.

"…mmm-hmm," he mumbled as he began to write on the marriage license with a…??!! Was that really a quill? It was. The Justice of the Peace was dipping a quill in an ink well, and filling out the form. He saw Alben staring, and chuckled. "Belonged to my great-great-grandfather," he said. "He held this very same post, when the state of Louisiana was first formed." He went back to scribbling, then stopped, laid down the quill, and stared at the driver's license. He again picked up the quill and continued to scribble.

And mumble. "Alben J. Barkley... they only give us one blank for the middle name... ...born in Le Flore County, Oklahoma... on July 20... 1930."

Alben instinctively started to protest! She was born in '32. But Joey yanked and squeezed her hand. Hard! She got it. This kindly Justice of the Peace in New Orleans Parish, Louisiana, had just made her eighteen years old. In keeping with state law.

The judge got proper identification from Joey, finished filling out the documents, looked at the nervous couple in front of him and said with a smile, "Let's do this. I'm hungry for some gumbo! Now, young man, do you—Petty Officer 3rd Class Joey J. Thibodeaux—take this lovely thing here, to be your lawfully wedded..."

In seconds, it was all over. Joey slipped the pawn shop marquis diamond on Alben's finger, and kissed his beautiful southern belle from Oklahoma, so long and intimately, the judge finally muttered, "Aw right, aw right! Get outa here. I wanna lock up."

They walked out on Chartres Street. It had turned cloudy and was still chilly.

"Hungry? Want some lunch?" Joey asked.

"No. I'm still full o' square donuts," Alben replied.

"Well, what d'ya wanna do?"

Alben looked up at Joey, said nothing, but her blue eyes beamed as she gave him a knowing, sensuous smile.

Shhrreeee! Joey's shrill whistle was so loud it hurt Alben's eardrums. But the green Checker Cab heard it and slammed on his brakes. "Hotel

Monteleone," Joey said; the only two words uttered for the five-block ride. He and Alben were too busy in the back seat, getting warmed up for the first few hours of their honeymoon in the comfy room.

CHAPTER TWELVE
Be sure!
Your sins will find you out!

7:32 p.m.

Joey aroused from his nap. Alben was still sleeping, naked atop the covers, by his side. He pulled the sheet over her so she wouldn't get chilly and went to shower. As he began to towel off, Alben opened the bathroom door, still naked.

"How long did we sleep?" she asked, a dreamy hoarseness to her voice.

"I dunno," Joey smiled. "Coupla hours? Damn! You wore me out."

"I think I need somethin' to eat. Gotta slight headache," she said, as she washed her face with cold water from the sink's faucet.

"Not surprised," Joey said. "We've had nothin' since the beignets. I'm starved. He paused before adding: "Course it could be the cheap champagne."

"I only had one glass," Alben quickly retorted.

"Like I said. It was cheap." Joey had ducked into the liquor store next door upon their noontime arrival at the hotel. "Did I drink the rest of it?" he asked.

Alben grinned. "What do you think?" She stepped into the still warm tub and turned on the shower. Moments later, she entered the bedroom with a towel wrapped around her torso. "I know you're gettin' tired of the only dress-up dress I brought, Joey. Sorry."

"Blue jeans will be fine tonight, baby. Just gonna take you to a li'l ol' joint I know, that serves the best gumbo in the world. "Then he laughed. "In fact, please don't dress too sexy. Don't think I'm strong enough for a night tonight …like this afternoon."

"We'll see about that," Alben teased.

She had just zipped up her jeans, which she had put on first, when Joey called from the window. "Look at this! It's snowin' in N'orluhns!" And it was. Fluffy white flakes drifted lazily down, and melted instantly when they hit the street.

"Great!" Alben cried, as a devilish little idea hit her. "Good weather for goin' to a little tavern. That is what it is, right?"

"Right." Joey was still looking out the window, which gave Alben ample time while his gaze was averted. She quickly put on her fanciest new, lacy brassiere—it was light blue—then immediately slipped on her red winter coat—no blouse! and buttoned the coat up. She also stepped into her pumps. She knew she would find the perfect moment, to shock and embarrass Petty Officer 3rd Class Joey J. Thibodeaux. She was determined, that Sailor Joey was not nearly as much worn out and done with romance on his wedding day, as he thought.

9:10 p.m.

They were back on Bourbon Street—Lafitte's Blacksmith Shop Bar. Joey told Alben this was supposed to be the oldest, continuous bar operation in America. (He also told her he wasn't sure that was true). They had managed to snag a back corner booth and each had already downed a huge bowl of gumbo with handfuls of oyster crackers. It was as good as Joey said, chock full of spicy andouille sausage. And the beer was cold. A hearty meal on a chilly night.

Joey and Alben sat close together, talking largely in the language of love: mere smiles and glances, punctuated with a kiss from time to time. They got up and danced often, kicking up their heels to the dixieland; then, sticking together like glue and moving intimately—even provocatively— when the sultry blues prompted. Then they would return to the booth and, upon occasion, talk seriously as to their future. What next? Did they have enough money between them to buy two train tickets to Portsmouth, Maine? Yes. Well, close. At least to Boston. Coach—no Pullman berths. But they better leave New Orleans soon, or they wouldn't! Where would they get the money for food and an apartment when they got to Portsmouth?

Joey, sheepishly, had another poker story. He said yet another acquaintance—a Navy captain at the Portsmouth shipyard—also owed him money, and he was sure he would get it. Because the officer would want no stink raised about such a thing. Navy officers aren't supposed to fraternize with enlisted men in the first place. Joey assured Alben the poker earnings from the captain would cover a month's rent and adequate staples, for at least a week or so. Alben was beginning to think Joey spent most of his spare time at cards. That part did not make her feel good.

"We can do it, Alben." Joey kissed her on the nose. "I promise."

His words again brought a smile to Alben's face. "I believe you, Joey," she said. "I believe you." And she kissed him on the lips.

"If I could interrupt you two lovebirds." The waiter set two new frosty mugs of beer on the table. "The boss. He see that mighty pretty diamond there. Thought y'all had to be newlyweds. All the beer ya want tonight, on the house!" The waiter smiled, bowed, and left.

"Uh… "—Alben seemed puzzled—"that waiter didn't talk funny."

"Whaddya mean?" Joey asked.

"I don't know. A lot of 'em seem to twist their tenses, and phrases all up… or somethin'. I don't even know how to say what I mean."

"Oh," Joey laughed, "those are the Cajuns."

"What does that mean?"

But before Joey could explain, the band struck up a raucous dixieland tune, and Joey and Alben took a big gulp of beer, and were back on the dance floor, doing moves they didn't know they knew. For fifteen continuous minutes they thought they were Fred Astaire and Ginger Rogers.

"Whewww, I'm burnin' up," Alben gasped as she slid into the booth.

But Joey was staring at the front door of Lafitte's, a frown on his face. "Who was that?" he asked.

"Who was who?" Alben responded.

"Some guy. He looked familiar. But I can't recall where I saw him. He was staring at us. Then he walked out. "

"Aw, who cares?"Alben was fanning with her napkin, and thought it the right moment to do her little theatrical exposé. "I need another cold beer. And I gotta get out of this coat."

Joey was still staring at the front door.

"Help me with my coat, Joey. "

He turned to see his new bride, half out of her red winter coat—no blouse—in a sexy blue bra. "Alben, what are you doing?"

She responded with a trill of laughter and Joey was no longer concerned with the guy who had just left Lafitte's. "Aw, come on. No one saw me, but you, Joey." She again pulled her coat around her.

"Don't be too sure, you little scamp! The look is quite fetching, though."

The waiter dropped off another beer for Alben. She downed half of it in one swig. "But I do need to get out of this coat, Joey. It's so hot in here!"

"Well, it's obvious that somethin's hot in here," he grinned. "Is this your way of sayin' you wanna head back to the Monteleone?"

"Yesss," she whispered.

The newlyweds were not ten feet inside the Monteleone lobby when Joey tightened his grip on Alben's hand. "That guy again!" he whispered. "The guy back at Lafitte's. "

"Where?"

"Here he comes. "

The man was obviously trying to cut them off before they got to the elevator.

"Dear God!" Alben exclaimed in a hushed voice. "It's Mister Scribner!"

"Who?"

"From the soda shop, in Heavener. He got on the *Southern Belle* ahead of me, when I left Thursday. But I never saw him after that." Alben was close to hyperventilating.

"Mister Scribner," Joey said as he stuck out his hand, "good to see you again."

Scribner ignored Joey—and his hand—and spoke directly to Alben. "Miss Barkley, we need to talk," he said sternly.

"About what, sir?"

"Your parents are quite worried about you. And frankly we're all disappointed in your actions."

Joey was still at Alben's side, but Scribner continued to ignore him. He resumed his fatherly lecture to Alben. "They found out I was down here to visit my ill stepmother, thought you might be here—and called to ask that I keep an eye out." Scribner turned abruptly and motioned to a man who was standing alongside the hotel desk clerk. As the man approached Scribner continued. "This here is Mister Crawford, the house detective for the hotel. He has also been on the telephone with your parents, and knows that I have their authorization to put you, young lady, on the very next train for Heavener."

"Mister Scribner," Alben began tentatively; then her voice became more firm; steady. "I don't believe you've been formally introduced to Joey—my husband—Petty Officer 3rd Class Joey Thibodeaux."

Scribner appeared startled as Joey reached in his hip pocket and pulled out their marriage license. "You and Mister Crawford might wanna look at this," he said calmly. Alben now stood with her arms folded, the marquis diamond in plain view.

Both men stood scanning the document, the detective taking reading glasses from his breast pocket for a closer look. "This looks quite authentic," the detective said quietly to Scribner. "I know Justice of the Peace Dupré quite well."

"Could we call and talk to him?" Scribner asked.

"I—I would want nothing to do with that," the detective responded. "If you—or the young lady's parents—want to pursue this, I would suggest you acquire legal counsel." The detective turned on his heel and walked away.

Scribner handed the license back to Joey and stared at Alben. "You at least should give your parents a call. You owe them that. They've been worried to death." He walked off at a fast clip toward the lobby's revolving door."

"Mister Scribner," Alben called—and he turned back. "You're right, sir. "A tear rolled down her face. "I've been very selfish… and thoughtless… in that part. I promise I'll call."

Scribner nodded without smiling and walked through the revolving door into the night.

Joey did not mention it to Alben, but was fearful Mister Scribner might have gone over the head of the concierge, and talked to upper management. Would they in the next few moments be kicked out of the hotel?

Apparently, no such thing had happened. The key to their room worked fine. There were no calls from the front desk. No ominous knocks on the door to escort them into the hall. After fifteen minutes, Joey began to breathe easier, and Alben picked up the phone.

She sat on the bed, her heart in her throat, as she heard the phone ringing in Heavener, Oklahoma. She heard the weary tension; the worry, in her mother's voice when she answered. Alben swallowed. "M-m-Momma?" she managed.

"Oh, Alben! Where are you?" Mrs. Barkley's voice contained both relief and fear. "Are you all right?"

"Yes, Momma. I'm fine." Alben struggled to keep from breaking into tears. "I'm—I'm in New Orleans... right now."

"You're coming right home! Right?"

"No, Momma. I—we're going to Maine?"

"What??!! Whose we?" More fear now in Mrs. Barkley's voice

"I'm married, Momma. "There was dead silence on the other end of the line. "I'm Mrs. Joey Thibodeaux, Momma. I'm sorry. Sorry I didn't call sooner."

"Oh, baby." Mrs. Barkley now spoke, barely above a whisper.

Alben could tell her mother was weeping.

"Alben, please. Here—talk to your father."

Alben could hear Mrs. Barkley talking to Mister Barkley—but could not make out what was being said. Then she could hear nothing.

Finally. "Your father does not want to talk right now." Mrs. Barkley sounded terribly sad.

"Momma, I'm sorry I hurt you—sorry you don't understand. But I love Joey. He's my husband, Momma."

Silence from Heavener, Oklahoma.

"I love you, Momma." Alben began to softly sob. "Momma, I… I saw Uncle Alben get sworn today. (sob) In a newsreel, on that new picture-box thing. (sob, sob) They have a new television station here in New Orleans." (more sobs)

Nothing from Heavner.

"Tell Daddy I love him."

Nothing.

"Goodbye, Momma. I—I'll call. Or write a letter. Soon." Alben could now barely speak through her own tears, as she added, "Hug F—Fred the Dog for me."

And there would be nothing else from Heavener—save the hum and crackle of the long-distance line.

Alben hung up the phone.

The newlyweds undressed in silence. Alben slipped her sheer nightie over her head, down across her naked body. Her actions were like a robotic automaton.

Joey lay on his back, staring at the ceiling.

Alben turned off the lamp, and crawled under the covers.

They did not speak. They did not touch.

Alben silently cried herself to sleep.

###

In the wee hours of morning, Alben was awakened by Joey's arms softly encircling her waist. In the darkness, he pulled her to him, and began softly kissing her neck and shoulders. Eventually, she turned to face him… and returned his kisses—tentatively at first; then, second by second, with accelerating passion. Breathing heavily, she rolled on top of Joey, continuing to kiss his face, his eyelids, his lips. Finally, she sat up on her knees, straddling his torso.

At 4:51 a.m., in New Orleans, Louisiana, the honeymoon—with soft moans escaping from each—was again underway.

Inexperience notwithstanding, some things you learn quickly. It's in the genes.

CHAPTER THIRTEEN
Do Not! ... Look Back

Twenty-four hours later—
Monday, January 24, 1949—
Somewhere in the Carolinas

Outside the moving train in the early morning hours, the weather was cold; intolerable for anyone without a coat. But it would have been laughable to describe it as a winter morn to any resident of the Portsmouth–Kittery area. And that's where Mister and Mrs. Joey Thibodeaux were headed.

The Piedmont of South Carolina had long ago served as hunting grounds for American Indian tribes; mostly the Cherokee and the Catawba. Now, its low rolling hills were home to small towns, and farms, which raised tobacco and livestock. It was common to hear a hillbilly or Appalachian gospel song pour from the radio; but just as normal to hear mournful blues from descendants of slaves, or something quite native to the region called "the Carolina shag"; or the same big band and pop tunes danced to by the nightlife crowds in America's major cities. East, west, and central.

Southern Railway's famous streamliner, *The Southerner*, was boiling through the Piedmont at a comfortable seventy-two miles an hour. Moonlight was trying to stream through grey clouds, but was only half-successful. The streamliner braked to a stop at the Magnolia Street Depot in Spartanburg at 4:20 a.m. —precisely four hours late. Sounds of screeching brakes, and steam escaping from passenger coaches, caused Joey and Alben to awaken—but barely.

The newlyweds looked out sleepily through frosty windows into a bleak cold morning, the breath of passengers waiting to board quite visible from their mouths and noses. In the darkness, the soon-to-be travelers stood on the loading platform hunched over, as humans do in cold weather. As though that will make them warmer. The scene made Alben snuggle as close as she could to Joey. She shivered until he hugged her tight, and pulled the army green Southern Railway blanket, provided by the porter, up to their shoulders.

Throughout the night, sitting side by side in the roomy seats, Alben had snoozed with her head on Joey's shoulder for awhile; then would curl up in a fetal position with her head on his lap. Then it would be Joey's turn to drape himself over Alben—but that was more difficult for Alben, Joey being half again her size and more. Plus, when his face was on her shoulder near her ear, his snoring kept her awake.

Before they left New Orleans, the newlyweds had slept until about nine-thirty Sunday morning, then walked to Cafe Dumonde for a quick, simple breakfast. That's when they concluded they'd better save as much of their stash as possible. So they quickly packed and slipped out of the elegant Monteleone, with Joey managing a thirty-second whispered conversation and 'thank you' to the concierge. The proxy benefactor (and brother), for Joey's poker buddy in Portsmouth glanced around nervously; as though anxious to get the newlyweds on their way.

They walked to the Southern Railway station to save money. Taxis would be used rarely from here on out. Joey was gentlemanly, and carried Alben's one suitcase as well as his duffel bag.

"When's the next train to Boston?" Joey asked at the ticket window.

"Well, ordinarily you'd have a long wait. But as it happens, The Southerner is runnin' way late. Had problems with the first two engines they tried. Unusual. But they're all ready now. Leavin' in about twenty minutes. Unusual." The ticket man seemed hell-bent on repeating the word. "Unusual," he said again. "For *The Southerner* to be four hours late, I mean. "

Joey told the agent they might do some sight-seeing in Washington and New York since they had the time; so the man suggested they buy tickets for one leg of the trip at a time. He further suggested they take the Baltimore and Ohio Royal Blue Line from Washington to New York, and the New Haven from New York on to Boston. Joey had already figured the bus, would be the cheapest way, on to Portsmouth, New Hampshire. That was the city across the river, and the Maine state line, from the naval yard.

Though he didn't mention it to Alben, Joey thought the sight-seeing in Washington and New York City might help their tiny nest egg. If they wandered the streets in the two big cities, they'd be worn out. They would sleep better when they got back to their coach seats on the train. And, it would get Joey a couple of days closer to the next Navy payday in Portsmouth; just in case the Navy officer who owed him, wasn't quite flush when the newlyweds arrived. Joey did not want his only recourse to be, slipping Alben into the barracks in the middle of the night.

Now, in the cold dawn which was yet to break, *The Southerner* slowly left the Spartanburg depot. The train snaked across the bridge that spanned Lawson's Fork Creek, which lazily flowed to the Pacelot River. In less than five miles—before the streamliner reached highball speed—Joey and Alben were once again asleep.

8:55 a.m.

The Southerner rolled to a stop at the Danville depot, the coaches—for some unknown reason—jerking more than usual. Which again awakened the newlyweds. The train had yet to make up any time.

"Danville," Joey said sleepily, reading the marquee. "Guess we're in Virginia," he added with a yawn. "Think I read somewhere, this was the last capitol of the Confederacy. The last—or next to last—can't remember which."

"Really," Alben responded, just as sleepily. There was little evidence in her voice that she cared at all about this, or any other capitol of the Confederacy.

Alben and Joey held hands as they gazed out the window in a zombie-like trance: that feeling one has when you're more asleep than awake. Because the only sleep you've had, is occasional bouts of slumber between depot stops; and the flickering red lights and clanging bells of railroad crossings. The night-shrouded lights and sounds are seen and heard over and over—sometimes vividly, sometimes barely—through coach windows, misted over by fog and dirt. Coaches that rock slowly from side to side. Sometimes lulling one to a delightful, peaceful plain; sometimes making one almost nauseous.

The Southerner pulled from the Danville depot, still moving slowly until it cleared the city limits. As it moved through a lower middle-class neighborhood, neatly manicured, Alben spotted a white frame house along the railroad tracks. Speckles of morning sunlight shone through barren tree branches on a yard of thick grass, still brown in the January chill. A girl, about twelve, wearing a red and black plaid mackinaw, was in the yard chasing (and being chased by), a pup at play. The girl was probably heading off to school, but would have preferred to stay home. In fact, she was probably already tardy at this time of day; or maybe she's playing hooky, Alben thought. The frisky pup's little tail twirled wildly. Alben could see, but not hear, the dog barking. And, yes it was. It was a snow white Lab-mix, just like Fred the Dog. She glanced at Joey. His head was back against the cushion, his chair in a slight reclining position, his eyes closed. That made it easier for Alben to wipe away the tears trickling down her face before he noticed. For a brief moment—though it would have been so thoughtless and doubly unfair to Mrs. Barkley—Alben wished she would have brought along Fred the Dog. But she didn't. And here she was, headed to Maine or New Hampshire, whichever it was. It was a place she'd never been, and barely heard of before Joey. Alben could not help but wonder what would happen today in her own class—the junior class—at Heavener, Oklahoma High School. She would be counted absent today …and forever.

###

It was an hour and fifteen minutes later. *The Southerner* had just left Lynchburg, Virigina, holding steady to its four-hour tardiness. Joey turned to look at Alben as she stared out the window. She was terribly quiet—understandable, considering this sudden change in the world of a sixteen-year-old girl—but he thought there was one problem he could solve. Because he needed it solved also.

"Alben," he asked, "are you hungry?" They had been very frugal with their small amount of cash—they had eaten one Baby Ruth candy bar apiece, since their Cafe Dumonde donut in New Orleans twenty-four hours ago. Joey felt light-headed from hunger. But Alben had uttered not one complaint, knowing how short on cash they were.

"What?" she responded quickly.

"Are you hungry?"

"Starved," she choked, tears brimming in her eyes.

"Come on." Joey led her down the aisle toward the rear of the train. "I think the dining car is only two coaches back," he said. Thrift was one thing; strangling the buffalo on the nickel another. But their faces dropped as they entered the dining car. "Oh no," Joey moaned, as there were no diners at all—only waiters polishing silver and wine glasses, preparing the tables for the next meal.

"Breakfast's over," said one waiter. "Sorry. Lunch about eleven."

"Any food in the club car?" Joey asked.

"Ah!" the waiter smiled, "the bartender will fix ya the meanest ham and cheese sandwich on the planet—if ya talk real nice to him."

That's all Joey and Alben needed to hear. The club car was full, the blue haze of cigar and cigarette smoke so thick it hung like fog from one end to the other. At least two poker games and one game of gin rummy were underway. The would-be card sharks were sipping Bloody Marys and Mimosas. Some were drinking coffee, but from their bloodshot eyes one might assume those all night players were making it through the morning with a shot of "Jack" in that coffee.

Joey pointed Alben to the one empty seat at the bar and leaned across the bar beside her.

"What'll ya have, sailor?" The bartender was a light-skinned Negro with blue eyes and a brilliant smile.

"We're famished," Joey replied. "Can't wait for lunch. Hear ya do a fine ham and cheese here."

"Only for the U.S. Navy," the man winked, "and only then when they have a pretty girl on their arm." He was already turning to the refrigerator, reaching for a small platter of sliced ham and a fresh block of cheese, wrapped tightly in cellophane.

"You a Navy man?" Joey asked.

"Battle of Midway," the bartender replied, his back still to Joey. "I was on the Yorktown. Wound up in the 'drink.'"

It was only then that Joey noticed a big scar on the back of the man's neck; a burn scar. It looked as though the scar continued well below the shirt collar.

"Glad to be alive." The bartender was still smiling as he set two

"Dagwood-style" sandwiches in front of the newlyweds. "Just… glad to be alive," he concluded.

"How much?" Joey asked.

"Three bucks and forty cents."

Joey put a five and a one on the bar. "Keep the change, sailor."

The bartender's eyes opened wide at the tip.

"And the drinks are on me," said the man sitting to Alben's right. "Give 'em whatever they want. As much as they want."

"Yes, sir, Mister Norris." The bartender spoke to the man with an abundant measure of deference.

Joey and Alben thanked the gentleman profusely, and ordered Bloody Marys.

The man was eyeing Alben's ring finger. "You two look like you might be on a honeymoon."

"Yes, sir," they answered in unison. "And going to my new home," Alben added. She had tried to sound joyous, but feared she failed.

"And where's that?" Norris asked.

"Kittery, Maine—next door to Portsmouth, New Hampshire." This time it was Joey who responded. "I'm stationed there."

"Ah, yes," Norris responded. "The naval shipyard."

"You been there?" Joey asked.

"I saw it from a sailing yacht once. A friend of mine lives in the area with his family. They've been in Portsmouth for years; and his ancestors before him. They love it."

The newlyweds finished their Bloody Marys, and without asking, two more appeared on the bar. "Thank you," they both mumbled shyly.

"Most welcome. Do you have much of a layover in Washington?"

"We might see a few sites before we head on," Joey replied.

"I'd like…" Alben hesitiated, then plunged ahead. "I'd like to see someone famous." She blushed as she name-dropped. "Mister Barkley—the new vice-president—he's my great-uncle."

"Really?" Norris's eyes went wide with surprise.

"Yes. I'm named after him," Alben continued. "My daddy is his nephew."

"So… your name,"—the man was putting this together in his mind—"is your name Alben Barkley?"

"Yes. Well, that was my maiden name. I'm now Mrs. Joey Thibodeaux." Alben felt her face flush again, speculating that Mister Norris knew he was looking at a couple who had eloped. Maybe even questioning whether they were actually married.

At that moment, the conductor of *The Southerner* entered the club car and Norris abruptly left his seat at the bar, to have a whispered conversation with the trainman. The conductor—grim-looking—nodded his head, and left.

An icy fear began in the pit of Alben's stomach. "Joey!" she whispered. "I think we're about to get kicked off the train."

"What?" Joey turned to her, as though she'd lost her mind. "What are you talking about?"

She whispered the imaginings she had just had, but Joey laughed.

"Come on," he said, "we've already been through this." He again pulled their marriage license from his hip pocket, waving it at her.

At that moment, Norris was at their side. "Very nice to meet you both," he said. "Congratulations—and again, sailor, thanks for your service to the good ol' USofA."

"And thanks for the drinks. " Joey replied, shaking the man's hand. Norris then exited the club car.

"Joey, I'm still nervous," Alben whispered. "Let's get outa here. Go back to our coach."

"What's wrong with you? They can find us as easy there, as here. Besides, we have paid-for tickets," Joey said, fishing the stubs from his pocket, and waving them also in her face. "Enjoy your free drink, Baby."

Twenty minutes later, the newlyweds arrived back at their seats, hunger pangs satisfied—at least for the moment—and a little drowsy from the drinks. They settled in for the rest of the journey to Washington, Alben finally beginning to accept Joey's assurances that her fears of being thrown from the train were paranoid.

Until thirty seconds later when she saw the conductor enter the coach from the front. The conductor slowly walked down the aisle toward them. He looked at each face as he walked until his eyes landed on Alben and Joey. Thereafter, he looked at no one else until he stopped aslongside their seats.

"Sailor, sir. Ma'm," he said. His face was expressionless. "Would you follow me, please." He walked on toward the rear of the car.

Joey looked at Alben, a frown on his face. She began to tear up. "I told you," she whispered hoarsely. But they both got up and followed the conductor. The trio walked slowly toward the rear of the train, through three cars and into the fourth—a Pullman sleeper. Midway down the aisle, the trainman stopped at a door, took a ring of keys from his belt, and unlocked the door. As he pushed the door open he stepped back, and with a smile, motioned them inside. "Mister Norris thought this Master Bedroom was a little more suitable for a young Navy man and his lovely bride on their honeymoon. The room was unbooked all the way to Washington and now it's yours; one of our finest, complete with a private shower. Plenty o' hot water. Mister Norris wanted you to have it, compliments of Southern Railway."

The newlyweds were shocked into stunned silence.

So the conductor continued. "We'll be in Washington in about three hours; but take your time. It'll be another couple of hours after we arrive, before the cleaning crew gets to this coach. You'll awaken in plenty of time, 'cause it'll begin to get chilly in here after the heat is disconnected."

Alben and Joey entered the magnificent Pullman accommodations, as though in slow motion, not believing their good fortune. The bed was already turned down, the crisp white sheets glistening off and on, as sunlight intermittently streamed through the window. A silver urn, filled with ice, stood by the bed. It contained a bottle of champagne, a frosty moisture visible on the upper third of the bottle. Two crystal flutes were secured in slots, along the urn's silver rim.

"Who…"—Joey's spoke as though in a dream—"who is… Mister Norris?"

"Sorry. I thought you knew," the conductor replied. "Mister Earnest E. Norris. He's the president of Southern Railway. And a very patriotic man. Enjoy yourself." Then, with a twinkle in his eyes—"Try to get some rest—or whatever." The conductor closed the door and left the newlyweds to themselves.

CHAPTER FOURTEEN
"…the Lord God formed
man of the dust of the ground…
and… God said, It is not good that the
man should be alone…"
Genesis 2:7,18

Ninety minutes later

Alben was peering out the window of the fast-moving streamliner. She stood there naked, hands against the window's narrow sill to brace herself. She could not believe the good fortune the railroad president bestowed upon them. She thought she should be taking advantage of the comfortable bed; she should be sleeping as Joey was. But she was not sleepy. Perhaps their just-completed, hour-long love match had been rest enough.

The beautiful Virginia countryside whizzed by outside the window, the rolling hills awaiting spring, longing to be green again; the ever-present blue mist hanging over the mountains at the far edge of the horizon. Then, the train slowed suddenly, and seconds later *The Southerner* came to a stop.

CHARLOTTESVILLE, read the station marquee.

Alben was in a virtual trance, dreamily watching the people move about on the depot platform; passengers heading for their coaches, others departing the train. It did not occur that her "live au natural portrait" in the Pullman window was visible to them.

Until! The eyes of a young man in the full-dress uniform of a United States Marine suddenly locked with Alben. His handsome face broke into a cautious grin. Shocked to reality, Alben grabbed a blanket from the bed and wrapped it around her naked body. She looked again at the Marine who was still smiling at her. She could not resist. She gave him a flirty little smile and a wink, before falling onto the bed alongside Joey. He stirred only slightly, drew her to him beneath the covers, and both fell into peaceful slumber. As *The Southerner* slowly left Charlottesville, the Pullman rocked back and forth ever so gently; a huge enveloping cradle for two young lovers, on the adventure of a lifetime.

...sometime, Monday afternoon...

Joey's eyes opened slowly. For five or six seconds he didn't know where the hell he was. Then he recognized the Pullman bedroom and realized the train had stopped. His arms and shoulders atop the blanket were cold. They must be in Washington. He eased from the bed, not waking Alben, and his assumption was confirmed as the first thing he saw looming out the coach window, was the recognizable dome of the U. S. Capitol building a quarter-mile away. The sky looked cold; grey. It appeared their Pullman was already detached from the train and on a siding. That meant the cleaning crew could be here anytime!

"Alben, baby, get up!"

She just moaned without moving, then pulled the covers over her head.

"Get up, sweetheart. We need to scram before the cleaning crew gets here." What time was it? Where was his wristwatch? He spotted it on the small built-in desk next to the bathroom door. 3:02. Had he wound his watch since leaving New Orleans? He hoped so. It was still ticking. 3:02 p.m. That should be right. He did recall rolling the watch ahead one hour to eastern time, while drinking Bloody Mary's in the club car this morning. Hopefully, he also wound the watch. To make sure he wound it again.

"What day is it?" Alben mumbled from beneath the covers.

"Uh… can't think. GET YOUR PRETTY ASS OUTA BED!" Joey yelled, laughing as he ripped the blankets from Alben's naked body.

"Damn, Joey. It's freezing in here!"

"Where'd a Church o' Christ girl learn to cuss like that?" he cracked.

"From my Catholic husband!" she shot back.

He scooped her up in his arms and carried her the few steps to the bathroom. "Splash some cold water on your face," he instructed. "Hell, I wanted to take a hot shower on the train. Never done that. But we gotta go. Water's probably cold by now, anyway, since the car's unhooked. We'll shower when we find a hotel."

"Together?" Alben asked. She turned from the wash basin with a teasing smile as she put toothpaste on her brush.

Without a word, Joey in one leap was behind her. His arms encircled her, his hands caressing the front of her body, from her neck down to her thighs. And back up again. Then back down again.

That's when the light knock came on the door. Joey had thus far managed to pull on only his undershorts and one sock; so he opened the door a mere crack and peaked around.

"'Scuse me, Mister Barkley. This here's the last room we got to clean… just wonderin'…"

"Sorry," Joey mumbled, "we thought we had more time. Give us ten minutes."And he closed the door.

"Welll!" Alben chortled, the words barely understandable through the toothbrush and laughter. She was going to enjoy this! "Good afternoon… MIS-TER BARK-LEY!" she gasped.

"Get your clothes on, smartass!" Joey groused. Apparently the crew had gotten word of the relationship to the new Vice-President; they had just missed which one was related to The Veep. "By the way, smartypants," Joey continued as he pulled on his trousers, "I just figured it out. It's Monday, January 24th. You're makin' fun of some poor slob whose trying to be nice, and treat you like a big shot. Just 'cause your cousin or somethin's the vice-president. And you don't even know what day it is." He ducked as he finished the sentence, because Alben had just thrown a roll of toilet paper at him.

CHAPTER FIFTEEN
Close Encounters Of
A 'Relative' Kind

Ninety minutes later

The hotel was just across Massachusetts Avenue from Union Station. The Commodore was in the 500 block of Capitol Street, NW. "They call it a workin' class place," said the newsboy. He was hawking the Washington Star. Joey bought a copy for a nickel.

The room was clean. Tiny. But cheap. There was barely room for the door to open without hitting the bed, which was pushed against the wall on the other side. There was a large window next to the bed with a sheer curtain; no blind to pull down. The headboard was against a wall, and once again, there was just enough room for the bathroom door to open at the foot of the bed. The bathroom was roughly four feet by four feet. No bathtub. Just a narrow shower, a small commode, and a smaller sink. No towel rack. Two clean towels, two clean washrags lay atop the water tank of the commode.

Alben immediately stripped, and went to shower. Joey tossed the front page of the *Star* on the bed and went to the sports page. Moments later Alben emerged from the bathroom, wrapping a towel around her naked body. Her wet hair fell in long chestnut waves around her face, and down her back.

"Gosh," Joey said softly, "are you offering dessert before supper?"

Alben gave him a flirty smile with raised eyebrows, which said 'maybe.' She picked up the newspaper. "Look!" she exclaimed, "there's Uncle Alben!"

"Dear Lord," Joey growled, "already! Here we go. "But his curiosity was piqued. He moved next to Alben on the bed to look. The photo was below the fold on the front page, and it showed a long table of smiling gentlemen, with the new Vice-President at the head of the table. The caption said Mister Barkley was the guest at a special luncheon earlier today in the Senate dining room, where he was feted and congratulated by old Senate colleagues on his new post.

"Be fun if we could see him," Alben mused.

"Yeah. Yeah it would," Joey agreed. "But unlikely."

Despite the grey skies, the day was rather nice, for Washington in January. Lower fifties, not windy. They decided to go for a walk before supper. Joey, of course, dressed in his Navy blues with peacoat. Alben donned her jeans, New Orleans sweater, saddle shoes, red winter coat and matching tam. Joey grabbed his Kodak box camera, and moments later they were walking up the steps on the Senate side of the Capitol.

Alben was awestruck. "Never dreamed I'd ever be here," she said. "Frankly—never thought much about such a thing. "

"I always wanted to come here," Joey responded. "Don't know why. Just did. "

A capitol policeman stood in front of the towering doors. "Sorry, folks," he said with a smile. "Already closed for the day. You can come back tomorrow."

The newlyweds, slightly disappointed walked down the long steps enjoying the view of the Washington monument. They reached the sidewalk and stood there marveling at the sights which in their existence, had been only from magazines, newspapers, and history books. A siren pierced the air to their left, and a motorcyle officer rolled to a stop virtually in front of them. Following was a long black '49 Chrysler. Joey recognized the model immediately, because the Admiral at the Long Beach Naval Yard had recently been assigned a new ride. It was virtually identical: a Crown Imperial eight passenger sedan.

This car was empty except for the driver. Then from a narrow corridor beside the steps to their right, came four men, headed right toward them. Two portly men were flanked by two capitol policemen.

Alben, with a gasp, immediately recognized one of the entourage. It was her great-uncle Alben. Joey recognized both of the dignitaries. His new great-uncle by marriage was with Speaker of the House Sam Rayburn of Texas.

Both men tipped their hats to young Alben, and Rayburn said "Evenin', sailor." The driver of the Chrysler was already holding the back door of the car for the officials.

Just before the men entered the vehicle, it was Alben who shocked everyone, including herself. "Uncle Alben!" she called loudly.

The Vice-President hesitated, turned around, and came back. "Ma'm?" he said.

"I'm sorry, sir." Alben's face was the color of her coat. "I'm so embarrassed," she laughed. "But my father is Herman Barkley, vice-president of the First State Bank in Heavener, Oklahoma. His father—my grandpa—is your brother."

"Well, I'll be darned!" The Vice-President's eyes widened. "Sorry I haven't kept up, uh… haven't kept up with family as I would've liked."

Young Alben thought she saw a hint of sadness in the Vice President's eyes.

"But I do remember hearing that one of my nephews went out west." He took Alben's hand into both of his. "And who's the young sailor, here?"

"This is my husband, sir. Petty Officer 3rd Class Joey Thibodeaux."

Barkley grasped Joey's hand. "We thank you for serving," he said—then turning to Alben, "I didn't get your name, sweetheart."

"Er—same as yours," she said shyly. "My parents named me Alben James. 'James' is mother's maiden name."

"Well, doggone," said The Veep. He turned to The Speaker who was waiting by the Chrysler. "Sam, you ever heard such a thing? My nephew named his daughter after me."

"Could've done worse," Rayburn cracked.

Joey had stepped back from the group and was snapping one picture after another, with his ever-present World's Fair Kodak.

"Get over here, Mister Speaker," Barkley called to Rayburn, "let's get a picture with my niece."

Joey snapped three times as the two old gentlemen posed, with the charming young Alben between them. Then, upon his bride's insistence, Joey gave the camera to her, so he could pose with the two famous politicians.

"Here, young lady." Barkley pulled a calling card from his coat pocket.

"There's the address of my suite—my office here in the Capitol. Mail me your address and that of your parents. I'd love to drop y'all a note. I'd talk more, but Sam and I got a meetin'—and I'm not just name-droppin'. Gotta go down to 1600 Pennsylvania Avenue, to confer with ol' Harry. Apologies," the vice-president chuckled, "can't stop callin' him that. He's 'Mister President' now. Goin' on four years."

The two piled into the back of the Chrysler, the driver gunned it—then screeched to a halt. Alben Barkley, Vice President of the United States of America, rolled down his window and shouted, "Sailor, my boy. You did mighty good there. Your bride looks just like Ava Gardner!"

The newlyweds, glowing inside, walked hand in hand from the Capitol grounds. Alben James Barkley Thibodeaux wore a smile that lye soap could not have washed off. My first letter home to Momma, she was thinking, will be very easy to write. I might even call her on the telephone. No. No, I'll write. Then I can send copies of Joey's snapshots.

CHAPTER SIXTEEN
A Ghostly Experience

The next morning...

7:22

Is it possible to inwardly sense that someone is staring at you? Even when you're alseep? Alben awakened with her face toward the hotel window—the one with the sheer curtain, no blind. The sound of the swishing street broom in the alley had awakened her. She was at eye-level with the man using the wide broom. And he was no more than three feet away through the window pane. He was not looking at her now... and he did not look her way thereafter. But in her mind, she was convinced he had been looking at her. While she slept. She was under the covers now—but had she always been? Or had the man seen her in the altogether as she twisted and turned in her sleep? The whole idea gave her the creeps.

Alben quickly slid from beneath the covers and out of the window's sight line. "Get up, Joey," she said softly, running her fingers through his hair. She now knelt on his side of the bed, away from the window. "Let's go see the sights, before we have to leave." She thought it best not to tell him her suspicions about the street sweeper. Joey might take it as a complaint about the room. And she knew that was the best they could afford.

"Hrgggpfth-uh," was all she got from Joey. And the last of the "response" was covered by a brief snore. But by the time she stepped from the shower, he was shaving at the sink.

They bought coffee and split a cinnamon roll in The Commodore coffee shop. They sat in a leather-upholstered booth by the window and looked out on a beautiful winter day. It looked as though it was seventy degrees, but "Huh-uh," said the waitress. "It was thirty-nine the last time I checked."

"Hey, Joey"—Alben suddenly remembered something—"I been thinkin'."

"Sounds dangerous," Joey teased.

"No. Really. Those bartenders in New Orleans; the ones I thought talked funny. You said they were Cajun. How come you don't talk like that? Mixin' words and tenses all around."

"Third and fourth grade teacher," he responded. "Sister Maria Elizabeth. She got it out of us. Made us speak English right—for better or worse. She was only 'bout twenty-five. And too dern cute to be a nun."

"Well! Is that anyway to talk 'bout a nun?" Alben demanded. "I s'pose you flirted with her too! Just like you did me!"

"So do you think that's… any way to talk 'bout a nun?" Joey shot back.

"Screw you," Alben whispered.

"Okay," Joey shot back… and laughed all the way to the cash register to pay the tab.

Moments later the newlyweds, shivering in the crisp breeze, stood at the base of the Washington Monument. "Shall we climb to the top?" Alben asked.

"Naw. Too much like boot camp," Joey replicd. "Didn't have to climb that many stairs, but too much sweatin', even when it's cold. Let's walk over there. "He was pointing to the north. The recognizable mansion was a mile away: the White House.

"The ol' house looks pretty good since Harry fixed it up. "The man who spoke behind them was a national park ranger in uniform. "It was a mess when he and Bess moved in. 'Bout to fall down. Rats runnin' 'round."

"Rats?" Alben shivered. "Are you serious?"

"Sure am. The Trumans lived across the street at Blair House for a long time. The carpenters had to gut the White House."

"Yeah, Blair House," Joey chimed in. "I remember that. Ain't that where the Puerto Ricans tried to shoot Truman?"

"That's right," said the ranger as he turned to continue his rounds. "Be sure to see the Lincoln Memorial." The ranger was pointing to the west. "That's spectacular. My favorite."

The couple decided to follow his suggestion and see Ol' Abe before trekking to the White House. When they arrived at the foot of the marble steps they paused to catch a breath before ascending. The temperature had warmed to the point that Joey threw his peacoat over his arm.

"Go all the way up and stand at the foot of the statue." Yet another park ranger spoke at Alben's elbow. "It's so real… it looks alive. "

Alben smiled at the man—then did a double-take! The ranger— now walking up the Memorial steps—looked identical to the one at the Washington Monument. Was he a twin? Or did he follow them here? She turned to Joey, but he had noticed nothing. Joey was mesmerized, lost in his own thoughts, staring back at the Washington Monument—and on past to the looming shadow of the Capitol. Alben turned again to watch the agent climbing the steps—and what she saw… or thought she saw!… made hair stand up on the back of her neck! In the exact spot where the agent should have been, there was indeed a man climbing the steps. But this man wore a long black coat. And a tall, black stovepipe hat!

Alben gasped! She was sure Joey would hear her. But he hadn't. He had moved a few yards away, closer to the Reflecting Pool, and had seen nothing she saw. She looked again at the long marble stairway—and saw no one. No park ranger. No tall man in a stovepipe hat.

Hand in hand, the newlyweds ascended the staircase and stood at the foot of Honest Abe. Alben was short of breath; not from the climb, but from nerves on edge at what she had just experienced. I'm tired from the trip, she thought. Need more sleep.

The ranger—or whoever; or whatever—was right. The bearded face of The Railsplitter looked like a man alive. The sculptor (the brass placque identifed the artist as Henry Bacon), had a gift. If you stood silently for a few seconds, you seemed to see the huge marble figure breathing.

A half dozen times throughout the day, Alben started to tell Joey what she thought she saw on the Lincoln Memorial steps. The tall man from nowhere with the stovepipe hat. But she did not. Joey knew he had married a sixteen-year-old girl. She did not want him thinking the little girl from Oklahoma still believed in ghost stories and fairy tales—even if she did look as grown up as Ava Gardner.

CHAPTER SEVENTEEN
Meeting Nellie Bly

Thursday, January 27, 1949

The streamliner *Nellie Bly*, of Pennsylvania Railroad fame, was boiling across New Jersey to New York—up the line from Atlantic City. The newlyweds had chosen this all parlor-car train, because it was ready when they were ready.

They had left Washington two days ago on the PRR's afternoon *Congressional*, after hours of walking the streets of the nation's capitol. Both Alben and Joey were enthralled by the old city whose buildings and monuments paid tribute to the seat of government in this New World city. The Founding Fathers' experiment in liberty and self-government was ongoing; sometimes faltering, but still going. That seemed to come from God's blessing and the intuitive sense of an electorate, that at times seemed more intelligent than the people they elected. When the representatives they sent here, got "too big for their britches," the homefolk set 'em straight and sent 'em back home. Of course, that didn't happen as oft as it should.

Joey had been so inspired by their Washington experience, he insisted they stop off in Philadelphia. He just had to see Independence Hall. They had stood in front of the magnificent Georgian building on Philadelphia's Chestnut Street, talking in hushed tones. They didn't have to. It just seemed the proper way to converse. This spot on God's green earth deserved reverence.

And that was even more their attitude once they moved with the tour group inside the old building, which had been completed in 1753, as the state house for the Province of Pennsylvania. They stood listening to the tour guide reveal they were standing in the same room where the Second Continental Congress had birthed the Declaration of Independence; where the Constitutional Convention had—with even greater labor pains—created a constitutional democratic republic: small 'c' …small 'd' …small 'r.' It was called the United States of America.

They heard for the first time—at least neither remembered hearing it before—that Abraham Lincoln had addressed a gathering of distinguished citizens in this very same room. He was en route to his presidential inauguration in 1861, never to return alive to this place, or to his beloved Springfield.

Before they headed back to their inexpensive boarding house—two blocks away, on Ionic Street—they saw Congress Hall, next door to Independence Hall, and again felt a shiver up the spine. The tour guide told them they were standing in the once-upon-a-time U. S. Senate; the very room where President Washington and Vice President Adams had been sworn for their second terms; and where President Adams and Vice President Jefferson had been sworn for their first.

"Wow!" That expressed everything Joey was feeling as they stepped out onto the sidewalk.

"Yeah," Alben responded. "I've always hated history—but wow!"

Another guest at breakfast, at the Ionic Street boarding house, had regaled the table that morning with his previous night at the Club Harlem Ballroom, across the Delaware River, in Atlantic City, New Jersey. "The singers and dancers are every bit as good, as what I've seen in the real Harlem," the man said.

"Wanna go?" That's was Joey's question to Alben now, as they stood on the sidewalk at Independence Square.

"How do we get there?" she asked.

"Robert what's-his-name—the guy at breakfast—he said there are regular buses to there, from the depot."

"Do we have the money?"

"I… think so." Joey was slowly calculating their stash in his head. "If we grab a cheap hotel there tonight, then head straight for Portsmouth. We'll have to do New York City some other time. When we got more dough. But I wanna get on with it anyway. Find us a little apartment in Portsmouth. Don't you?"

"Sounds nice. "

As adventurous and exciting as all this was, the newlyweds were feeling something else: a desire for stability and normalcy, in this new, spur of the moment, impulsive life. A life they had bargained for—for better or worse.

"Do you think…?" Alben began. "Do you think they'll let me in? The club I mean. In Atlantic City. I'm just sixteen."

"Of course, they'll let you in," Joey grinned. "You look like Ava Gardner!"

###

At the Club Harlem Ballroom, they had 'danced their buns off.' Just like in New Orleans. But even more so. As they moved on the dance floor, Joey had watched Alben, as she watched the professional Negro troupe. He was astonished at how she instantly mimicked their bluesy struts.

"You're amazing!" he said.

"What?" she yelled. It was hard to hear over the music.

"You're amazing!" he yelled back. "Your moves!"

"It's easy," she grinned, "when you're havin'!... so!... darn!... much fun!!"

###

The *Nellie Bly* was crawling along now, a quarter-mile from Union Station in New York City, and Alben was reading a Pennsylvania Railroad pamphlet, taken from the back of the seat in front of her. It was about the real *Nellie Bly*. Of how she was a woman ahead of her time:

In the 1880s, a seventeen-year-old Elizabeth Cochran had written a response to a sexist editorial. It had appeared in the *Pittsburgh Dispatch*. But—she did not sign her name. It was signed, "Anonymous." The editor was so impressed by the writing, he placed an ad in his paper, for the author to come forward. And appearing before him, was the teenage Elizabeth.

Despite no female reporter at his paper—maybe nowhere—she talked herself into a job. However, the editor demanded she write under a pen name. She chose "Nellie Bly."

'Miss Bly' became a great undercover reporter. It was on to the New York World, and in 1889 and '90, inspired by author Jules Verne, she traveled around the world, reporting all the way. To celebrate her feat, the Santa Fe Railway christened a one-time, super fast train from San Francisco to Chicago, to help Bly best Verne's fabled '80-day' world trek, in just 72 days. They called it the *Nellie Bly Special*.

Thus, decades later, the Pennsylvania Railroad paid tribute by naming this very train—the train they were now aboard—for the pioneering female journalist.

"Hmmm." Alben lifted her eyes from the brochure. "Joey?"

Joey turned to look at his teenage wife beside him as the *Nellie Bly* moved slowly into Grand Central Station. She had a teasing smile on her face, a dreamy glaze in her eyes.

"Joey, do you think I'll ever have a train named after me?"

"You already do," he answered. "It brought you to me. *The Southern Belle*."

CHAPTER EIGHTEEN
Home Sweet Home…
A Long, Long Way…
From Home

Portsmouth, New Hampshire
Saturday, January 29, 1949
2:20 p.m.

"Whaddaya think?" Joey asked quietly, as the apartment house manager stood ten feet away. The woman was forty-five-ish, pleasant, and good-looking. In a cheap sort of way.

"I… it will do. Fine, I think." Alben knew the facts. This was about money. Or the lack thereof.

The former inn on Bow Street was run down. Even seedy. There was no other way to put it. However, there were now eight small apartments in the old building, and this two-room apartment on the second floor had recently been vacated. Therefore, the walls sported a sparkling coat of brand new paint. And the linoleum floors had been scrubbed spotless. That made very obvious how worn the linoleum was; but one can handle worn, if clean. The furniture that came with the place was just as worn as the linoleum; but again, would do. They could—they would—make this home.

They had arrived at the Portsmouth bus depot twelve hours ago. Alben had groused a little when she stepped off the bus. "This ol' Portsmouth bus depot ain't quite like the Boston South Station, is it?" Boston South was where they had alighted from the New Haven Railroad, and trekked the few steps to the bus.

"Naw," Joey laughed. "I think whoever built Boston South was a limey."

"A what?"

"A limey. A Brit. Some English architect designed that. At least that's what it looks like to me. I had a buddy at the Los Angeles base. He'd been to London and had snapshots of their grand railway stations. Magnificent."

Then, in Portsmouth, the newlyweds had first grabbed a cab in the undercover driveway of the bus station, and stepped out of the vehicle in front of a motley hotel, on Market Street; right on the bank of the Piscataqua River. That was the first moment Alben experienced the damp, frigid, two a.m. January "breeze" of an Atlantic coastal town.

"Oh… my… God!" she whispered, hoping Joey didn't hear. Heavener, Oklahoma winters were no picnic—but this! The wind had cut through her red winter coat and blue jeans as though she were naked.

Now, their new apartment—their new home—was within easy walking distance of that drab hotel. Both spots were within a stone's throw of the 'breezy' Piscataqua. Alben wondered if she'd have to buy long underwear. The thought creeped her out. She could not imagine Ava Gardner in long underwear.

Monday, February 1, 1949

Joey was due back from leave, at 0700 hours. He arrived at the naval yard at 0630, wanting to look up the officer who owed him poker money. He found him, saluted smartly, and had his plea downpat. "Sir, I'd surely appreciate it if I could have the eighty bucks from our game three weeks back. Uh, sir… I got married while I was gone. And, sir… well—I really need it. With my bride here and all."

"Sailor, I was hoping to get a little more even. In another game. That's the way we usually…"

"I understand, sir. But… uh… I had to rent an apartment, of course, and…"

The young officer stared at Joey sternly, then smiled. "Of course, sailor. Meet me at the commissary on your noon break, and I'll have it for you. And congratulations. "

"Thank you, Sir." Joey saluted again and turned to leave, feeling much relieved.

"Sailor?" the officer called, "is she pretty?"

"As a picture, sir." Joey flashed a wide grin. "She looks like Ava Gardner."

"You lucky swab," the officer laughed.

CHAPTER NINETEEN
Novice Fashionista

Summer, 1950

It was a few short blocks from the Bow Street apartment, to Robertson's Jewelry & Finery Shop. The walk to Congress Street was very pleasant for Alben—except when it was raining cats and dogs, (or in the winter, which seemed colder than her imagined North Pole). So much had happened in the year-and-a-half, since the newlyweds arrived on that winter night.

Within their first ten days in Portsmouth—though Joey had said nothing worrisome to Alben—she knew: he was concerned, and Alben was certain it was all because his Navy check could not possibly stretch as far as necessary. She had given up on going back to high school; and Joey no longer mentioned it either. Without telling him, Alben decided to look for a job. She tried the nearest grocery, and the nearest dime store; no checkout or stock girls needed. Then, on her third day of the job search, there was a sign in the window at Robertson's: FEMALE CLERK OPENING— FASHION SENSE HELPFUL. Alben had no experience whatsoever for such a position, but she was convinced she had all that was needed. Don't I look like Ava Gardner?

She immediately returned home to reapply makeup and press her only 'dressy dress'; which she was already wearing. She pulled on a fresh pair of hose and found Joey's black shoe polish to shine her pumps. Then, she brushed her teeth again, and sprayed on heavy shots of perfume. She got as far back as she could from the floor length mirror, leaning against a corner of the bedroom, and walked toward the mirror over and over; trying to determine how much exactly, to sway her hips. Slightly seductive, she told herself, but short of a 'floozy'. Mister Robertson interviewed her for seven minutes—and hired her on the spot.

There were some months Joey and Alben barely had the rent, but somehow, they made it happen. And could even—most of the time—scrape enough together every couple of weeks to have a night out at one of the half-dozen bars Joey and his fellow sailors patronized. Just beer and hamburgers, and dancing to the jukebox. But it was fun.

Within Alben's first six weeks at Robertson's, she had overheard a conversation with an acquaintance of Mister Robertson. It had piqued Alben's interest.

"You seem mighty happy today," Robertson had observed. "Did you win the Irish Sweepstakes?"

"Heavens, no," the woman replied, " but I am proud of myself. I just got my GED."

As Alben listened, the woman described the twice-weekly classes, the long hours of home study; but the woman glowed as she confessed the jubilation that little certificate brought. She knew then and there, that—would be Alben James Barkley Thibodeaux's next project. Eight months later, and fourteen-thousand times of falling asleep on the couch late at night (as she lost her place in the textbook), Alben had the coveted GED. It meant another occasion in which she genuinely looked forward to talking to Momma back in Heavener. And Momma was indeed delighted, as Alben knew she would be.

The young couple did not have a telephone, but Alben tried to call home every other month from the phone booth in the nearby drugstore. Long distance calls were just too expensive to call more often. She also called on her birthday in July, to thank her parents for the ten-dollar check they sent; and she called them on Thanksgiving and Christmas. Her parents sent her a fifteen-dollar check at Christmas; addressed just to her, not Joey. And Alben had shipped small presents to her parents: a silver money clip for her father; a tiny bottle of French perfume for her mother. Both came from Robertson's, where Mister Robertson told her to take her time, paying off the credit account he had set up for her. Alben also included with the gifts, her mother's beautiful silk scarf she "borrowed" when she left on the *Southern Belle*, thanking her for the warmth it provided. Each time her mother wrote, she seemed a little more concerned about her baby girl. However, Mrs. Barkley was proud of the snapshots with Vice-President Barkley and Speaker Rayburn; and of the "lovely handwritten note the vice-president sent me and your father," her mother wrote. "I framed it; and hung it right by his picture in the living room. Of course, I hung the snapshot of you, the Veep, and Mister Sam right below it." Alben's mother didn't mention the fact that Joey had taken the picture; or that Alben also sent a snapshot of Joey between the two national leaders. In fact, Mrs. Barkley seldom mentioned Joey at all.

But there had been one subject that prompted a couple of letters back and forth: the romance of the year, that caught the attention of the nation. The Vice-President of the United States of America fell in love. And for a seventy-one-year-old widower, he did quite well. The gal he wooed was a comely thirty-seven-year-old widow from St. Louis, Missouri. He met Jane Rucker Hadley at a Washington party, some four months after becoming

Truman's "Veep." His airline romance with the St. Louis beauty caught the fancy of the public, including Alben, her mother, and even Joey. When the Veep put a ring on Ms. Hadley's finger at a St. Louis altar, she was thirty-eight—and the Vice President was just shy of his seventy-second birthday. The date was November 19, 1949.

For all this happy distraction, there was one thing that pierced Alben's heart to the quick: her father had spoken to her on the telephone only once. At Christmas, just once. He had said exactly thirteen words: "Merry Christmas, Alben. Wish to hell you'd get yourself home. Here's your mother." That was it.

Alben tried to hide it from Joey. But Joey knew anyway. Alben was terribly homesick, Christmas, 1949.

CHAPTER TWENTY
Storm Clouds

June 26, 1950

There was a paperboy each morning on the corner near Robertson's, and he always called out the top *Portsmouth Daily Herald* headline, in the most melodious sort of way. In recent days, his sing-song chant had often been about Korea. And Alben had noticed that Joey, every evening—the moment he walked in from the shipyard, he turned the radio to news. He'd listen to Gabriel Heater, then Alex Drier, then Morgan Beatty. It was national network news; and it was mostly about Korea. Joey would say little to Alben. Until the news was over.

"Joey? Are you worried?" Alben had asked.

"About what?"

"The news. You… you seem obsessed."

"The news? What's that got to do with me? I'm just interested in what's going on," he answered with an air of indifference; but his indifference was not convincing.

Things began happening fast. It was on this Monday morning that the newsboy's voice seemed more mournful: "KOREAN DEFENDERS DRIVEN BAAAAAA-aaaack." he chanted. North Korea had invaded the South. A day or two later, a U. S. Navy patrol boat sank a North Korean troop ship, with 600 soldiers on board.

A day or two after that:

"U. N. ORDERS MILITARY SANCT-iiiioooonnns," the newsboy sang.

And on the first day of July, 1950, Alben felt a chill, that made her break out in a cold sweat.

"TRUMAN COMMITS TROOPS

TO KOOOORRRRR-EEEEEE-aaaaaa!"

Thursday, August 17, 1950

Alben was first delighted—then a foreboding. This evening as he entered the door of the apartment, Joey announced big plans for the night. "Let's go get dinner. Someplace nice. How 'bout Warren's?" he said. "Call a cab." No Gabriel Heater, no Morgan Beatty; no network news of any kind.

She knew. Something was afoot.

The lobster stew at Warren's Lobster House in Kittery was as tasty as ever—but Alben was not enjoying it. She knew the other shoe was about to drop.

It seemed to affect Joey also. Instead of devouring his sirloin steak in normal fashion, he moved it about on the plate with his fork. "Alben," he began—"Alben, the orders have come through."

She waited.

"I'm shipping out." Joey's eyes expressed the desolation that Alben instantly felt. But that's all he said.

"When?" she finally asked.

"Tomorrow evening. 1800 hours."

Alben felt she had taken a battering ram to the solar plexus. She felt nauseous. She had thought a month, maybe—at least two weeks. But tomorrow! She ate not another bite.

"But why you?" she asked. "You're... you're an electrician."

"Sweetheart," Joey responded, "subs need electricians, too. Besides. I—I'd feel better about myself, if I did my part in this little Korea dustup."

However, Alben saw something in Joey's eyes; something he was not saying. Was there more to his assignment? More than just being an electrician? She started to pry; but knew it would do no good. Finally, after another two minutes she spoke. Softly. "Let's go home, Joey."

"Yes," he replied. "I thought about that; thought you might wanna go back to Heavener. I don't blame you."

"No!" she shouted; and was embarrassed by the stares of other patrons at Warren's. "No," she continued in a softer tone, reaching over to touch his cheek. "Not to Oklahoma. I just mean here. Now." Tears trickled down her cheeks. "Our home, Joey. Our home. On Bow Street."

And they did. Home to their bed. For what they knew would be the last time, in a long time, they made love. Slowly. Passionately. And slept in each other's arms.

CHAPTER TWENTY-ONE
Farewell

The next evening, with the sun low in the west, Alben stood on the bank amid the other wives and girlfriends. She couldn't be sure, but thought she spotted Joey waving near the conning tower of the USS Odax. Whether it was him or not, she fixed her gaze on the sailor as she tried to hold back her tears. The combined tears of all those lovely young things, waving their hankies—some frilly, some plain—numbered well into the thousands. The millions? Who could know?

In moments, the Odax had slipped away into the fog of the Piscataqua River and the waiting Atlantic.

Hours later—
Fifty miles off the coast of New Hampshire

There is no way Alben could have known this; in fact, Joey had no specific knowledge of what was about to happen—but he knew much more than he told Alben. He was now dozing, sitting up on a bunk, in the over-crowded submarine.

"Attention!" A Navy Commander had appeared in the oval passageway. "Mickleson. Shelton. Thibodeaux. This is you. To the conning tower. The Odax is surfacing."

As Joey stepped onto the deck of the sub, he welcomed the cool night air and the starry sky, after the stifling confines of the underwater craft. He immediately noticed the dark outlines of an approaching boat, with only three small running lights; and those were dimly lit. As the craft pulled alongside, he caught enough of the lettering to know it was a Coast Guard cutter. A gangplank was extended to the sub's deck, and the three sailors boarded the cutter. The craft immediately turned back from whence it came, and with full throttle, roared into the night. But ninety seconds later, the pilot backed the motors off to almost nothing, and pulled alongside a towering aircraft carrier. They passed right beneath the lettering of the carrier: USS Cabot, it said. Joey had been concentrating so intensely on the millions of stars aloft, he had completely overlooked the looming ship.

A rope ladder dropped from the carrier onto the deck of the cutter, and the three sailors were shortly aboard. Conversation was scarce. "Over there," a carrier sailor motioned, pointing to an R7O-1, the Navy version of the Lockheed Constellation. Joey and his companions were hustled up the narrow metal stairway, and were just in the process of buckling their seatbelts, when the plane's four motors roared into life, throttles completely up. The plane quivered as the pilot waited for the signal to release the brakes.

Can this thing actually fly off an aircraft carrier? Joey wondered. It could. However, Joey's stomach and heart were in his throat when the plane sagged toward the Atlantic, as the carrier's short runway ran out. And why all the diversionary secrecy? he wondered.

Joey had no precise knowledge; but he'd heard enough scuttlebutt, he thought he knew where they were headed: the San Francisco Bay area.

With a couple of fuel stops, of course, en route. From there he could only guess. But he had a good idea.

CHAPTER TWENTY-TWO
Loneliness And... Temptation

Two months later
Mid-October, 1950

It was a slow day at Robertson's Jewelry. Mister Robertson had told Alben it was a good time to polish the 1847 Rogers silverware on display in the front window. "It's something that needs to be done every couple weeks," he said. "We must keep it looking tip-top, if we're going to sell any."

Alben actually enjoyed the task. It was wonderful, to handle such dining room finery; to make it look even better than it already was. She wondered if she would ever own such. And with pangs of homesickness, remembered that her mother did. Back in Heavener, Oklahoma.

Of an evening, in Joey's absence, she would often drop by Hilyard's Drugs a half-block from the apartment, and have a chicken salad sandwich; or a hamburger and coke. It was too lonely in the apartment to cook for herself. She would sometimes pick up a sultry romance magazine for a nickel at the newstand. Just to pass the time. They were filled with sordid, melodramatic stories of pining, passionate war wives, weary of the wait for soldiers and sailors; boyfriends and husbands, absent from the beds of the lonely girlfrends and wives. It was mere entertainment; something to pass the time as she ate. I'll never be that sort of cheap, slutty wife, she thought.

Then, one afternoon, Alben noticed a young man standing in front of the display window on the opposite side of the entrance, looking at

Robertson's variety of necklaces. He was not in uniform, but still wore the telltale white sailor cap and navy blue peacoat. Yet another naval enlistee off duty. A moment later she recognized him: the young sailor who had imbibed a bit too much at a USO dance, a week before Joey shipped out. The one whose open flirting had made her uncomfortable—yet thrilled her at some level.

The sailor looked up, gave Alben a startled smile of recognition, then a hesitant wave. She smiled back but was praying he'd go away; yet hoping he wouldn't. He solved the dilemma by opening the door and entering the store.

"Hello," said the sailor.

"Hi. May I help you?" Alben responded in her most professional manner.

"Not really. I... I just remember you from the USO dance. Awhile back."

"Oh, yes. Yes. Right." Alben was doing a less-than-stellar job of pretending she didn't remember. "How have you been?" she concluded weakly. "I don't know your name."

"I'm Herbie. Seaman Apprentice Herbert G. Green, officially," the sailor added with a grin.

"I'm Alben. Uh... may I show you something?" Alben was feeling like a shy, bashful little girl in front of a new boyfriend, the feeling suddenly compounded by her realization that what she had just said could be interpreted as naughty. If the sailor so wanted. Sailors were very good at such, she had learned.

"No, no. Uh... I heard your husband was sent to Korea."

"Oh, did you know Joey?"

"Not well. We have a mutual friend. Have you heard from Joey?"

"Once. About a month ago. When he first boarded his assigned sub. And they won't even let him reveal it's name. He warned me that his letter-writing would be infrequent."

"Where is he?" the sailor asked.

Alben shrugged. "I don't think he even knows for sure. Said he'd guess they'll be patroling the Yellow Sea and the Sea of Japan."

"Well. Glad you're okay." Seaman Herbie said, then appeared to be unable to think of anything else to say. "See ya 'roun'," he concluded, and quickly exited the store.

Herbie dropped into Robertson's once a week for the next couple of weeks. Sometimes it was just a Hi, how ya doin'? moment. Then—at about the third week—he began to show up every day or so. He told Alben he had been tapped for the enviable job of running errands for the top brass at the naval yard; ferrying dry cleaning back and forth; buying their special cigars and booze, whenever the commissary ran short. That's why he was in town so often.

"Don't know why they picked me instead of an ensign," he said. "But I'm glad they did."

Herbie began to look at items of jewelry; friendship rings, necklaces and bracelets; and he revealed on one of those visits he had a new girlfriend, and was looking for a special gift for her. That revelation (Alben was ashamed to admit), gave her a slight tinge of jealousy. But on the other, she relaxed a little. There was nothing wrong with befriending Herbie. After all, he had a girlfriend.

Another couple of weeks passed, and as Herbie was about to leave Robertson's he said to Alben, "Uh... I know Joey is in Korea; but I don't think he'd mind. Since we're just friends... uh, would you—would you have dinner with me some night? Just as friends? I just like someone to talk to."

Against her better judgment, "I guess that would be.... okay," she said. "Just... friends... at dinner. Or supper, as we call it in Oklahoma. "She laughed, then added: "But wouldn't your girlfriend mind? You could invite her to come along, if you want."

"No, no. She won't mind," Herbie responded. "Really. Why should she?"

So it was, that Seaman Apprentice Herbert G. Green and Alben Thibodeuax settled on a 'date'—just as friends. A Thursday evening, one week before Thanksgiving, 1950.

CHAPTER TWENTY-THREE
Rendezvous

They were meeting at the Wayside Inn, a comfy little tavern and inn, a short block-and-a-half from Alben and Joey's upstairs apartment on Bow Street. They would meet there, have a little conversation, something to eat, and go their separate ways. That was all.

There were still debates in Alben's mind—debates with herself. She early on determined she would dress very plainly, so no one could possibly think anything was awry, even if somone saw her and Herbie together. But as it happened, the very Thursday of their dinner date, a shipment from the Paris house of Jacques Fath arrived at Robertson's. Included in the shipment was a silvery white silk blouse, matched with a black silk skirt. Both garments felt sheer to the touch even though they weren't; and the skirt, (which stylishly covered the knees), because of the design and slick fabric, the moment its wearer sat, the knees and three inches more were exposed.

Ever since Joey shipped out for Korea, Alben had spent much of her time—to combat loneliness and keep her sanity—following the world of high fashion. She had become a little obsessed with it, which pleased Mister Robertson very much. He knew little about such, but could readily see the uptick in sales in the ladies finery department, since Alben arrived. In appreciation, he did something he had done for no other employee before: he told her she could purchase anything she wanted for herself, and pay Robertson's a mere three percent above the invoice. And should then merely re-order the item for the store's stock. She had seldom taken advantage of his generous offer. Despite her intense interest in high fashion, she had no occasion to avail herself of the bargain. Until now.

Alben could not resist. Before she left the store that evening, the Jacques Fath skirt and blouse belonged to Alben. She had not been paying much attention to how she looked since Joey shipped out. Just how her customers looked.

As Alben got ready for her dinner engagement with Herbie, her conscience nagged a bit. But she was determined to enjoy an innocent evening with Herbie. She was doing nothing wrong. She needed this evening. She wanted to feel like a real woman again. And she wanted to make Herbie feel good. She appreciated his paying attention to her. It would not be fair to him, if I don't dress up. She should show proper respect for the kind invitation to dinner; just a dinner for two casual friends.

Alben, standing in front of the mirror, finished off her high fashion ensemble with a string of faux pearls around her neck, and a pair of matching earrings. She once again ran a hairbrush through her chestnut waves, and Yes! For the first time in weeks, she really felt she looked like Ava Gardner.

Since it was such a short trek for Alben, she threw only a dressy black shawl over her shoulders, and made the walk in the chilly damp air, in two minutes. Despite the tavern being close by, she had never been in the establishment. On the rare occasions she and Joey had been able to afford a night out, he opted to take her to one of the spots where his fellow sailors went—unless they really splurged and went to Warren's in Kittery.

The Wayside Inn was the quintessential New England coastal inn. Dim gaslights, with smoky glass chimneys; a dark polished mahogany bar and tables, and a tiny back booth, tucked in a corner under a stairway. The booth seat was on only one side of the table, and that was against the wall. It was so small, two people of average size could barely fit into it. That's the booth where Alben spotted Herbie after a few seconds of surveying the room.

"Hi," was all the shy seaman apprentice could manage as he rose to greet Alben.

"Good evening," Alben said clearly. She had dressed up as a lady… and By George, she was going to act the part on this night. She slid into the booth, and Herbie followed.

It was then that Herbie said something that erased all doubt in Alben's mind, that she was happy to be here. "Ohmigosh!" he sputtered. "Has anyone ever told you? You look just like Ava Gardner!"

"Really? Oh, pooh. Of course not," she protested, blushing bright pink.

It was not a question of Herbie trying to be fresh. It was plain that if the two of them were to sit in the booth, his leg would be pressed against hers. There was no other way.

"Cocktails before dinner?" the waiter asked.

"Yes!" Herbie replied instantly. "A scotch and soda for me. Alben, what do you like?"

Alben was taken aback. Excited, queasy—at how fast it all was happening. "I… I've never had a scotch… er… scotch and soda," she stammered, giggling. "What's… what's…?"

"No time like now to try it," Herbie grinned. He held up two fingers to the waiter.

Alben felt like every nerve ending in her body had converged upon the mid-section of her inner thighs, lower tummy, and every fingertip she owned. She believed that Herbie was just as on edge.

"How is it?" Herbie asked.

Alben had just had her first sip of scotch and soda. "Mmm!!" was her only response. But it was good enough that moments later, she readily agreed to a second round.

They both opted for the Wayside Inn special: a bowl of New England clam chowder, served with fish and chips. And a small loaf of Irish soda bread with farm-churned butter alongside.

They talked about little during the meal, except music: Herbie's love of the Tommy Dorsey Orchestra; Alben's love of hillbilly music out of Tulsa, and Texas, and of course, Tennessee.

"Never cared much for that stuff," Herbie confessed. "But with you? I'm sure I could get used to it." He reached over and gripped her hand.

It was the first time since she arrived that Alben felt really uncomfortable. And it was the first time she remembered neither had mentioned Joey. Or Herbie's new girlfriend.

Before she could verbalize her feelings—even if she'd had the courage to do so—Herbie signaled the waiter. "Alben, have you ever had claret?"

"No. What's that?"

"Just a light, French wine. Sort of a… oh… dessert wine, I guess. Virtually no alcohol," Herbie lied.

"Fine," Alben whispered; and knew Herbie was lying. She was having too much fun to care.

Herbie excused himself to go to the rest room. When he returned, it seemed to Alben that he pressed even closer to her in the booth. But how could one tell? It was such a tiny booth.

"I love that blouse and skirt," Herbie said, feeling of each as he spoke.

Alben just looked at him dreamily... blushing again.

"Uh...Alben," Herbie continued, "I... I think I should tell you. When I talk about my new girlfriend. I... I've really been talkin' 'bout you." He paused, looked directly at her, and seemed to inch even closer. "I mean... we're just friends. I know you're married and all... but he's... he's so far away. What's wrong with a little companionship?"

"Nothing," Alben heard herself say. They sat silent, eyes locked.

Herbie took her hand. He squeezed it lightly, lifted it from her thigh to his lips, and kissed her fingers.

Alben was shaking. She knew what was coming next, hoping it wouldn't; but hoping it would.

"I've just been thinking," Herbie said. He dropped her hand softly back to her thigh, but continued to hold it. One of his fingers started to slowly draw tiny circles on her thigh. Through the thin, silky, black skirt, it felt as though Herbie's finger was directly on her bare leg. An electric tingle went through Alben's body. "Wouldn't it be nice to... to just..."—(Herbie coughed a little)— "...to just sit and listen to some music. The rooms here... are very nice. Upstairs. Here. Very clean. Each room has a radio. I saved my money once, just so I could stay here on weekend leave. Just to get away from the naval yard."

"That... that sounds nice." It was as though someone else was speaking.

Alben didn't want to say it. She hated that she had just said that. It just came out.

"So… shall we just go on up?" He reached in his pocket and laid a door key on the table. "I made arrangements. Thought I'd just spend the night and listen to the radio, even if you didn't. I mean even if you didn't wanna listen to music for… for just a half-hour or so."

It would be so nice, Alben thought, so nice… just to sit and listen to music… and Yes, dammit! to be kissed. After all, I am a grownup woman… and soooo lonely. Alben knew she was going to say 'yes'. She would despise herself hereafter—but she knew she was about to say 'yes'.

In the end, she didn't have to say anything. Herbie put eighteen dollars on the table. An ample amount to cover the meal and drinks, plus an ample tip from anyone. Especially a poor sailor boy.

Herbie was holding her hand, his arm around her waist, as they started up the stairs. One… two…three… they were on the seventh step, when…

"Herbie!" Alben said. "… no. No! I can't. I'm sorry, Herbie. Please. Let go my hand." In a flash, Alben ran down the steps to the door of the Wayside Inn; down the street, and she tore up the stairs to her apartment; their apartment. She and Joey's. She fumbled with the key for a frantic fifteen seconds, seemingly unable to unlock the door. Finally, she did. Locking the door behind her, she threw herself on the bed fully clothed, and cried… and cried… until she fell asleep.

CHAPTER TWENTY-FOUR
New Life

If Alben had any regrets of ultimately rejecting Herbie's advances, they were soon gone. It was 12:35 the next afternoon at Robertson's: Alben had just waited on Mrs. Hottlettmeyer, a weekly customer, who had purchased yet another dress a size too small; a dress meant for someone much more svelte than Mrs. Hottlettmeyer would ever be again. Yet, somehow, Mrs. Hottlettmeyer never returned any of the 'too small' dresses. Maybe she paraded around the house in them all by herself; or maybe her husband enjoyed her trying to fit into them. Maybe he liked his wife in dresses that were way too tight. It is, after all, the thought (or the memory), that counts.

But in the next second, Mrs. Hottlettmeyer and her 'too small dresses' were of no concern to Alben. There was virtually no warning. She had to barrel full-bore, to the tiny rest room (For Employees Only), in the back of the store. Her hand over her mouth, she barely made it to the commode to vomit the entire contents of her stomach, into the porcelain.

A concerned Mister Robertson heard her wretching, and moments later tapped timidly on the rest room door. "Mrs. Thibodeaux, are you ill? May I help?"

"I... I'll be fine."Alben's weak voice was barely discernible through the door.

Mister Robertson's wisdom and insistence won out. He demanded that Alben accompany him across the street to his family doctor. Alben crossed the street—stopping traffic—leaning heavily on her boss's arm.

The good doctor was most gentle, but very thorough. "Did you say your husband was recently sent to Korea?"

"Yes, sir," Alben managed.

"Mmmm," said the doctor. "And when did he ship out?"

"Uh… let's see"—Alben could not think clearly—"seven weeks ago… tomorrow, I think. I think. Maybe eight. I… I have it marked on my calendar."

"Mmmmm," said the doctor. "Just lie back on the table and rest. I'll be right back."

Four minutes later the doctor returned with a cold washrag, placed it on Alben's forehead instructing her to hold it in place, then helped her sit up on the table. Alben tugged her fashionable pencil skirt down from mid-thigh, where it had remained following the examination.

"Mrs. Thibodeaux," the doctor smiled, "Alben, it is, right? Yes, of course," he added, answering his own question. "In the next letter you write your husband, tell Petty Officer Thibodeaux, that when he returns from the Korean theatre he can greet the third member of his family. You are carrying his child!"

At that very same moment—
Off the northeast coast of North Korea

Joey sat up in his bunk. He knew instantly what had awakened him:

the *USS Sea Devil* had cut its engines. The only movement was the natural float, as the submarine continued slowly in the direction the engines had been propelling; counteracted from time to time, by the currents of the Sea of Japan. In the dimly lit stillness, Joey was not afraid. Not really. But he felt very alone. Yes, he was still accompanied by his two comrades from Portsmouth. And all three had gone through the special training for this mission together. They now fit every definition imaginable of "blood brothers." And for a few moments longer, they were surrounded by the small crew of the *Sea Devil*. But. That was about to end. The trio of Portsmouth sailors would soon be on their own.

However, even that knowledge was not what made Joey lonely. It was knowing that his mother and father, his older siblings, (a brother and two sisters he hadn't seen in years), and most of all his dear Alben; dear, dear Alben. None of them knew where he was or what he was about to do. And it was unlikely they would ever know of this mission. His loneliness only increased as he realized now more than ever that he might never see any of them again.

He knew of nothing else he could do. However, before getting into the bulky, black insulated clothing and boots, which would likely still fall short of keeping him warm, he reached into the breast pocket of the garment and pulled out his rosary beads. He then prayed the Our Father, more slowly— and certainly more sincerely—than he ever had before.

CHAPTER TWENTY-FIVE
Still Of The Night

one hour later

Joey and his two comrades had never experienced a night so black. And, as they feared, it was brutally cold. Fortunately, the insulated wardrobe—for the most part—was doing its job. They followed the proper co-ordinates the best they could. It was Joey's job to hold the softly illuminated compass low in the thick rubber raft; the other two manned the oars. They had been told they were likely forty minutes from the shore, depending on the tide. They had now been rowing an hour. Joey kept glancing up from the compass, and there! Fifty yards ahead against the black sky, he caught the outline of something even more black: rough, jagged boulders—some huge, some not so huge. They had reached the North Korean coast.

The Portsmouth trio, about to set foot on enemy land, had only learned the final details of their mission aboard the *Sea Devil*, just hours ago.

In September—a couple of months ago—the *USS Perch* had deposited a group of Great Britain's Royal Marines at virtually this same spot. The Brits had successfully carried out their mission: to destroy a railroad train tunnel, which was a vital link in the Communist north-south supply line. The Royal Marines had lost one man in the process, who was buried at sea. However, NATO had received intelligence that a huge cadre of Chinese soldiers had been working diligently to rebuild the tunnel. Joey and his two buddies were charged with finding the spot, to determine whether the intelligence was accurate, and if so the trio carried enough TNT in their backpacks to disassemble a small mountain. Or a train tunnel. Hopefully, with a huge contingent of 'commies' inside.

As the Portsmouth sailors found a small cave in which to hide the rubber raft, many questions went through Joey's mind. Would they be able, with their very limited navigational equipment, to find this cave again? Would their small radio transmitters actually make contact with the Sea Devil, for a successful rendezvous at sea? Or would those radio signals merely alert the enemy of their position? Would these three blood brothers from the Portsmouth Naval Yard make it out safely? Or would one of them... be buried at sea? And if so... which one?

June 1, 1951

My dear, dear Joey,

I have not received a letter from you since mid-November. And that was only the second one I got. I still read both of them, over and over. But I know you are alright, and would write if you could. Or perhaps you are writing, and the mail is unable to get through.

But I am writing today with fabulous news. Sorry I did not feel up to it sooner.

Just ten days ago: May 22, 1951. Your beautiful, beautiful daughter was born. It hit me as I was being rushed to the delivery room, that we had never discussed names for a child. But I think you'll like the one I chose: she is Miss Jo Alben Thibodeaux. Her hair is black, but she has my blue eyes. 6 lbs, 2 oz, at birth; 19 inches long. And I tell her about you, every day. I know she'll love her daddy. She already does…

Alben then told Joey of her promotion to assistant manager at Robertson's Jewelry and Finery Shop. She didn't mention that she wondered how she could be anything else. After all, she was the store's only employee, except Mister Robertson himself. And, of course, Mrs. Robertson who came in every Monday to do the bookkeeping from the week before. But it meant a pay raise of fifteen cents an hour, and Alben was delighted to have it.

Petty Officer 3rd Class Joey J. Thibodeaux never received that letter from Alben. He received no letters from anyone anymore… and hadn't since stepping aboard the USS Sea Devil.

On this day, the grey light of early morning shown through the sole 1x12-inch window, covered by bars only, no window pane. When he stretched his arms as high as possible, he could barely touch the ledge of the concrete wall around the window. And the North Koreans had not been thoughtful enough to provide any furniture in his cell. Unless you counted the dirty cotton mattress on the even dirtier dirt floor—and a thin wool blanket which did not keep him warm, even though he slept in the shirt, trousers, and underwear he wore the night he first stepped on Korean soil. The thick insulated garments—basically coveralls—had been taken immediately from Joey and his buddies upon their arrival at the prison. He wished he knew more about the rules of the Geneva Convention, for he was certain there were numerous violations in this situation. But he only thought of such things to keep as much mental health as possible. It brought a rueful smile to his face, to contemplate there was no one to complain to. No matter the number of Geneva violations.

CHAPTER TWENTY-SIX
Date? Sadly, unknown...

On that earlier fateful night, Joey and his two buddies had been out of their rubber raft only thirty minutes when they found themselves surrounded by enemy soldiers, some aiming bright flashlights in their eyes; all aiming military rifles their way. And as a punctuation, the weapons had bayonets affixed. It was a quick, inauspicious end to their mission to say the least. It caused Joey to wonder if their attempt had been foolhardy at best. Had military intelligence totally screwed this up? Or was their capture inevitable, no matter what?

Now, months later, Joey could not be sure what day it was, but had tried his best to keep a calendar in his mind. One reason he could not be sure of the day, was that he and his Portsmouth comrades had been subjected to severe beatings many times, in the first several days at the prison. He knew he had drifted into unconsciousness over and over, and had no idea how long those periods might have been. Moments? Hours? Days?

The trio was interrogated repeatedly with glaring, white bright lights in their faces. They were always surrounded by a half dozen sullen and speechless guards, all North Korean or Chinese—Joey couldn't tell the difference—plus one Asian officer who was taller than the rest. He was the only one who ever spoke. The officer spoke to the guards in what Joey assumed was both Korean and Chinese, because he could detect a slight difference in dialect now and then. Of course, he had no idea what was being said. But the dialect variance was what made him assume there was a mixture of Korean and Chinese personnel present.

However, the tall officer spoke to the Portsmouth sailors in perfect English, complete with a British accent. The questions were just as one would expect: how did you get here, what is your mission, etc? And Joey was proud of his little band of brothers. To the best of his knowledge, despite the beatings, glaring lights, days without food—some days without water; the tall officer got nothing from the sailors except name, rank, and serial number.

For some reason, after many days (Joey could not even venture a guess as to how many), the beatings and interrogations had stopped. Sadly, so had any sightings or knowledge of his comrades. For all he knew, they were dead.

Although Joey tried to drive it from his mind, it was obvious that the severe treatment had taken its toll. He could not walk without a limp; a limp that seemed to grow worse, instead of better. It was not that he had immense pain when he walked. That part did seem to get better. But it seemed a muscle in his right leg, little by little, grew weaker.

He was led from time to time—maybe three days a week—to an outside area, 8x10 yards in size. When it was cold, it was cold! Some days so brutally cold, Joey was ready to return to his cell in three minutes. But he was afraid if he did not stay the full half-hour, he would never be brought outside again.

The outdoor yard was surrounded by double barbed wire on three sides. There were numerous strands of wire, no more than four inches between them, which stretched twenty feet high. That was on three sides of the "exercise" area. The fourth side, of course, was the stone wall of the prison.

Attached to that wall (in a very crude manner), was a basketball goal, sans net and backboard. There was a very old basketball always lying on the cold ground when he arrived, always in need of more inflation, which of course was unavailable.

Here, he was watched constantly by one or more guards standing in the corner of the yard. He could see no other buildings from the yard; no other people. Just an expanse of bare land which stretched as far as he could see; only two or three trees on the visible plain. His human contact? Just the guards. He could from time to time hear voices in the prison; but always far away, and always of oriental dialect. For all Joey knew, he was now the only prisoner of war in this compound.

However, on this day as the grey light in his cell's window turned brighter, Joey would have a celebration. Of sorts. It by necessity would be a mere mental and emotional celebration, dampened by moments of intense loneliness which cut like a knife. Nevertheless, by the calendar in his mind—however inaccurate it might be—this was July 4, 1951. And By God!! Joey thought, I am proud to be an American! They cannot take that from me.

CHAPTER TWENTY-SEVEN
Forsaken

It was a few days later that Joey awoke, hunger pangs as usual, after the meager soup and rice of last evening's prison "dinner." It took him a few seconds, but then he sensed that something was different. What was it? Yes. It was the total absence of any sound; of any human activity. None of the usual oriental accents, from faraway in the compound. Just the stirring of an occasional breeze outside; the sound of a few birds. Other than that—nothing. And when the time arrived for exercise, there was no guard to take him outside. Nothing. Joey had already feared as much.

He crept as quietly as possible to his thick, cell door and pushed gently against it, hoping against hope it would open. It did not. The outside bolt was as firmly in place as ever.

Joey sat down on his filthy mattress; shaken, scared, and as downhearted as he had ever been. He was always aware he might die in this prison. But there had always been hope. Now, for the first time, he had to face a real possibility: that he would die alone—right here in this cell—of starvation.

He reached for the only item of solace he'd been left: the rosary. He began to recite again, the prayers of his childhood catechism.

CHAPTER TWENTY-EIGHT
Ambition

Tuesday, September 2, 1952—
Portsmouth, New Hampshire

"Alright. Let's see. Now, I must see your high school diploma." The petite nun had a smile like a two-hundred-watt light bulb; her blue eyes, naturally large, appeared as big as saucers behind her thick glasses. Her cheerful disposition was not at all the image that Oklahoma-born, Church of Christ-bred Alben, had of a Roman Catholic nun. "You did bring it with you, I trust?" asked the beaming nun.

This was the moment Alben had dreaded. She hoped a GED certificate was acceptable. She had been led to believe it would be, but was anxious. "Uh… yes. Yes," and Alben hesitantly handed the cheerful sister the parchment-like piece of paper.

"Oh," the nun said slowly; even somberly, Alben thought, and her heart skipped a beat. Then, "That's fine! Here it is," the sister suddenly exclaimed. "The state seal is in a different spot than I've seen it before. Yes. Fine. We accept GEDs from the State of New Hampshire."

Alben breathed a huge sigh of relief. She had taken the bus from Robertson's this evening after Labor Day, to St. Catherine of Siena Church on Woodbury Avenue. The parish had just been founded a year earlier. Alben saw a write-up in the *Portsmouth Daily Herald* two weeks earlier, that the new church was offering a few extension courses, from St. Anshelm

College in Manchester on Tuesday and Wednesday evenings. They were encouraging adults to further their education. Three courses were being offered: History of the Christian Faith, Clerical Bookkeeping, and World Geography. It was the last one that piqued Alben's interest. She assumed her Joey was somewhere in or near Korea; but she had little idea of where that was, or why he had to be there.

St. Anshelm was offering the ninety-minute courses each of the two evenings, and a passing grade in any of the three subjects, after two semesters and an eight-week summer session, would be counted as college credit; just the same as taking the course in any accredited New Hampshire college for a full year. And through the benevolence of the church's outreach, the tuition for any course was a mere seven dollars per semester; five dollars for the summer session.

Three weeks in, Alben eagerly looked forward to each Tuesday and Wednesday. She became enthralled with geography, and in only the second session had asked the young priest who was teaching, to explain what was happening in Korea; why the country had become divided? Why was the U. S. military there? After the class ended, he had stayed an extra twenty-five minutes to explain, to the best of his knowledge, the basic particulars. Alben had almost missed her bus home; but made it to the bus stop with a mere sixty seconds to spare. She was now dreaming that maybe someday—when Joey got home—of finishing college, and teaching world geography in high school.

Alben and her mother were now corresponding regularly. They exchanged letters most every week. Mrs. Barkley included a line or two in each letter, urging Alben to come home to Heavener, now that Joey was off in the war. But Alben just as firmly resisted, saying Joey would be home soon.

Their increased communication was prompted in part, because dear Uncle Alben, in mid-1952—following President Truman's announcement that he would not seek re-election—had entered the race for President. Barkley even got the endorsement of Mister Truman—but all to no avail. The Democratic Convention nominated Governor Adlai Stevenson of Illinois.

Alben's mother was so disappointed; but young Alben was more philosophical. "Please, Momma," she wrote, "a President Barkley would be almost 80, at the end of his first term."

But her mother was not assuaged. She wrote back that she would probably vote for Eisenhower. And told her daughter, "Your father, Alben!—I'm quite sure, he'll vote for Ike." And her mother didn't stop there: "I can't imagine what my dear late father—Democrat sheriff that he was, in Texas County, Oklahoma—would think of his son-in-law. Let alone me, for marrying him."

CHAPTER TWENTY-NINE
Reality

August 5, 1953

Alben arrived home late. It was almost midnight. She had warned Faye Tompkins—the kind widow in her sixties, down the hall, who regularly babysat little Jo Alben on class night. Alben said she would likely be late, for it was the final class in the St. Anshelm geography class.

All went well, grade cards were handed out… and Alben got an 'A'. She teared up off and on the rest of the evening; tears of joy. She was proud of herself.

The small teaching staff—two nuns and one priest—held a reception for everyone after class in the St. Catherine parish hall. It was a delightful small affair, complete with champagne and cookies. Afterwards, Alben and two other students—young women her age who lived near Alben's apartment—got off the bus together, and decided to have a late night drink at the Wayside Inn. The three sat down at an out-of-the-way table, and Alben glanced nervously around the room. She inwardly breathed a sigh of relief, when Seaman Apprentice Herbie Green was nowhere to be seen.

Alben walked off the street into the foyer of her apartment building, and checked her mailbox. Disappointment again. No letter from Joey.

"Mrs. Thibodeaux?" It was a male voice at the top of the stairs, in front of Alben's apartment door. "So sorry, ma'm. Didn't mean to startle you. I told Mrs. Tompkins I'd just wait out here." The man wore the dress uniform of a Commander in the U. S. Navy. "Might I come in and talk to you a moment? Before Mrs. Tompkins leaves."

"Uh, yes. Yes, of course." Alben walked up the stairs, her heart in her throat.

"I'm Commander Elgin," the officer volunteered, as Alben inserted her key in the lock. "I… I worked closely with Joey at the naval yard, and…"

By this time, they were in the small living room, and Alben in robot fashion, motioned the officer to a chair.

"Dear?" Mrs. Tompkins spoke from the bedroom doorway. "Would you like me to leave?"

"No," Commander Elgin interrupted. "If you can, Mrs. Tompkins, ma'm—wait just a bit."

Alben was shaking as she sat down on the couch. "Why are you here?" she finally managed.

"As I'm sure you're aware, Mrs. Thibodeaux—everyone knows—the Korean armistice was official just a few days ago. So I'm now free to visit with you. We wanted to…"

"Is Joey okay?" Alben blurted, tears already filling her eyes.

"We hope so, ma'm," Commander Elgin said softly. "That's why I wanted to talk with you… in person."

The officer's hesitant approach was not reassuring. Alben clutched the wooden arm of her small couch till her hand hurt.

"We have not heard from Petty Officer Thibodeaux for—for some time, m'am." The officer was somber, his eyes displaying deep sadness.

"Nor I," Alben sobbed.

"I'm sure you haven't," Elgin went on, "but I hasten to add, we continue to hope he is well. And hope to hear from him soon. I apologize that we have not been able to tell you this sooner; but due to the sensitivity of the situation—we could not."

"What does that mean?" Alben asked. "Sensitive about what? Joey was just an electrician. "

"He was much more than just an electrician, ma'am." The officer paused. "I cannot yet reveal details, but I can tell you Petty Officer Thibodeaux volunteered for a special assignment—a very important one."

"Are you saying he's a prisoner of war?" Alben felt her blood turn to ice.

"Ma'm, in war… anything is possible. But with the cessation of hostilities, we're—we're hopeful we'll hear something soon. And pray it will be good news. I'm sorry there are not more specifics." With that, Commander Elgin stood to his feet and looked expectantly at Mrs. Tompkins.

The woman did not wait for him to speak further. "I'll stay with Alben for awhile," she said. "All night if she wants."

"Thank you both," Elgin replied. "I'll be in touch, Mrs. Thibodeaux." He stepped into the hallway and closed the door behind him, before returning his officer's cap to his head. He breathed a sigh of relief; which as usual, brought no relief at all.

CHAPTER THIRTY
Retracing Steps

Five months later—
January 21, 1954

*T*he *Crescent* rolled slowly across the causeway, bridging the vast expanse of Lake Ponchartrain. The conductor had just knocked on the door to say they were now a mere twelve minutes out of New Orleans Union Station.

The sun had already dropped out of sight in the west, but it was obvious the sky was cloudless. There was still a slight tint of bright orange at the horizon. From the sleeper window, Alben could occasionally catch a glimpse of an orange ripple; a reflection on the huge lake's waters from the sunset almost gone. But she had no idea whether it would be warm or cold when she stepped off the train. The window of her roomette was cool but not frigid. Would it be almost tropical, as it had been on that morning she met Joey in the "Big Easy?" Or would it be chilly, as he had earlier warned? All that—all that seemed ages ago.

It had certainly been cold when she left on the bus in Portsmouth, two mornings ago: two above zero, the thermometer had read at the Greyhound depot. She took the bus to Boston, where she boarded the New Haven Railroad, Train #177, to New York City. That's where she boarded *The Crescent* for New Orleans. The porter had led her to the roomette, for which she had scrimped and saved for weeks to afford. She was taking little Jo Alben—for the very first time—to visit both sets of grandparents. She thought the little enclosed space would make the trip much more comfortable for herself and baby Jo; not to mention the other passengers. Jo Alben was now two-and-a-half, but not beyond a wail or two (or three), if the mood struck her. Alben and little Jo would need to change trains and depots in New Orleans, to go to Rodessa and Joey's parents. Then on to Heavener to introduce her own parents to their very first grandchild.

Alben had so wanted to go home for Christmas of '53; but would not dare to leave Robertson's Jewelry and Ladies' Finery in the holiday lurch. She needed that job, and had insisted to Mister Robertson she would wait till after the first of the year, if he would then give her a three-week leave. Of course, no pay for the time off. "Would that be possible, sir?"

"Alben, are you ever coming back?" There was a kind, plaintive sadness to his question.

"Yes, sir. Yes, sir! This is my home until Joey returns. After that? Then, sir, it will be up to him."

"But Alben." Mister Robertson had a pained look on his face. "Do you...do you really think he's coming back?"

Alben's eyes had welled with tears. "I have to," she sobbed. "Joey"—she could barely speak—"Joey's never seen little Jo Alben."

"I'm sorry, Alben." Robertson put his arm around her shoulder. "That was stupid of me. Unthinking. I apologize."

"It's okay," she had blubbered through her tears. "I understand."

###

Alben did not have to wait until she stepped off *The Crescent*, to know this was no balmy day; nothing like the day she arrived in New Orleans, in 1949. As soon as she stepped into the passageway between the coaches, the cold blast hit her. This was the "freeze your ass off" New Orleans Joey had warned of.

Just after she stepped onto the platform, the friendly porter who had insisted on carrying the sleeping Jo Alben off the coach, handed the child to Alben. "Thank you," she smiled… and reached in her purse to hand him a ten-dollar bill.

"Oh my, ma'm… no. It's been such a pleasure. I didn't expect…" the porter seemed embarrased at the size of the tip.

"But I insist," Alben replied, "You've been very helpful the entire trip. And I'm just so happy to be here with my dear li'l girl."

"Thank you. Thank you, m'am. "

Another porter set down her luggage—all four pieces—in front of her. "Ya want me tuh take these inside, ma'm?"

"No, I need a cab to go to the KCS depot. "

"I'll getcha one, ma'am."

The cab was there in mere seconds. The driver loaded her luggage, and as they drove off, he pointed to the right. "Ain't that a pretty buildin'!" he exclaimed.

"Yes. Very modern," Alben replied. "What is it?"

"Oh, that's our new Union Passenger Terminial," he replied. "N'Orluns mighty proud o' dat. Mighty proud. Gonna dedicate it 'bout April, I hear."

Moments later the cabbie deposited his fares and luggage at the Kansas City Southern depot. Alben stood there for a moment as the cab sped away. For the first time in the entire journey it hit her. This! was the very day— January twenty-first! Five years ago, she—Alben James Barkley, a sixteen-year-old girl from Heavener, Oklahoma—had arrived in this intoxicating city to meet Joey. There was no getting around it. She had been a runaway southern belle, arriving on the Kansas City Southern's *Southern Belle*. To meet her wild sailor boyfriend. What the hell was I thinking?

Alben held her little girl close, rocking her gently back and forth, as she turned one way, then the other. Tears welled in her eyes. It was deja vu... but different. Five years ago, she had stood on this very platform and searched franticly for a glimpse of Joey. However, this time she was not frantic. She had no expectation of seeing Joey today. She held little Jo Alben even tighter as she rocked her back and forth on her shoulder. Was she now crazy? Delusional? To hold out that Joey was alive?

It was at this moment, that Alben's tears began to dry. This was the moment that somewhere down deep, she admitted to herself. She would never—never in this life see her darling Joey again.

CHAPTER THIRTY-ONE
..."Seeing Through A Mist Darkly"...

Five days later
January 26, 1954
8:24 a.m.
Rodessa, Louisiana

The sound of the *Southern Belle*'s airhorns! And the headlight of a KCS E1 diesel, an early model, rounded the bend a quarter-mile south.

"Oh, Mom and Dad Thibodeaux--thank you so much." Alben hugged her parents-in-law. "You've been so kind. And I can tell this child loves you as much as you love her. Sorry this trip is so short."

Happy tears rolled from Alben's eyes as she smiled at the child in her arms. "Oh, little Jo Alben," she cooed, "we're goin' home to see my Momma now. You'll probably call her Gram-ma-ma. And she—and my daddy—they're gonna love you so much. Just like me and your daddy love you." Alben by now had vowed it would be many years before she told little Jo that her daddy was not coming home.

Jo Alben's young round face beamed like sunshine, in response to her mother's hug.

The northbound *Southern Belle* rolled to a full stop, steam rolling from beneath the coaches. Alben hung back, making sure the porter got all her luggage to the train.

Then!

Something caught her attention. A movement. Someone had just stepped down from the *Southern Belle*. The very last coach.

She looked past Joey's parents to see a tall sailor. An officer in winter blues. He was carrying a single leather valise, and appeared rather old. His face was gaunt. He was extremely thin. She thought of Joey… but it could not be him. He walked with a pronounced limp. And a cane. The black visor of the officer's white cap shadowed his face.

"My dear, dear Alben. "

At least that's what Alben thought she heard. His voice was weak and frail as he limped toward her, leaning heavily on the cane.

"Oh, Alben!"

It was Joey!

A joyous cry came from Joey's mother, as she and Mister Thibodeaux ran to their son. Alben was right behind them, walking as fast as she dared while carrying Jo Alben. It was like a prayer circle, as everyone kissed and hugged everyone else. Neither Joey or Alben could speak. But they could weep. And they could hold each other and little Jo Alben, in the sheer joy and gratitude of the moment.

"Anybody goin' with us today?" It was the voice of the conductor, exercising as much kind patience as he could muster.

"Tomorrow. Or the next day," Alben replied, "or next week. But not today."

"PORTER!" The conductor motioned to the trainmen standing in the coach passageway. "Set the lady's luggage off. "

"Yes, suh."

And seconds later: "All a-boaRRRRD!" The conductor hopped onto the steps as the northbound *Southern Belle* began its slow roll out of Rodessa, Louisiana. On the station platform, the Thibodeaux family continued their surprising and joyous reunion.

And Alben looked forward to the next reunion very soon. With Mr. and Mrs. Barkley, Mr. and Mrs. Joey Thibodeaux, and little Jo Alben—and of course, Fred the Dog—all together in Heavener, Oklahoma.

EPILOGUE

...well, here I am again. This is Alben—the older Alben, who first introduced you to this little autobiography. At this point, I think I might be comfortable fininshing my story in the first person:

This short memoir has taken me longer than I thought. I did celebrate my eightieth birthday last week. It was wonderful. Mainly, because I took my driver's license test on that day—I needed to because of my age—and I passed with flying colors. I am glad, because at least once or twice a month I like to drive by that old first apartment on Bow Street. The building is still there, but now it seems that every six months or so, some business or another—a law office, a souvenir shop, a tailor—a business or two moves out—and others move in. But I bet in some rooming house nearby, there dwells a handsome sailor and some romantic little girl whom he's enchanted, and talked into marriage—and they make love every night. The story is repeated over and over, and I envy them. Who wouldn't? And who knows how many such stories are found in the cozy apartments along that precious waterfront?

I do want to fill in details of what my Joey told me after our glorious reunion:

I will never forget the joy I felt when he stepped off the *Southern Belle* in Rodessa, in 1954. I had given up hope. But there he was!

He was not in good shape. But he was home. We had a joyous few days with his parents in Rodessa, before Joey, Jo Alben, and I boarded the

Southern Belle for Heavener. My dad, the banker? Well, he tried two or three times to apologize for being such a hardass... (and he would hate that language from me), but I merely hugged him and said, "Daddy, think nothin' of it. If Jo Alben ever runs off like I did, I'll blister her butt!"

After a few days, Joey and I had a long talk in Heavener, and decided to return home. Our home. Portsmouth, New Hampshire.

"Sweetheart," Joey said, "I'm a navy man. I love the sea. I'd love to live...and die, in Portsmouth with you." He did not have to ask me twice.

And the POW days:

Even as I write these words, I cannot keep tears from eyes. He had indeed, been left by the commies to die of starvation. They had deserted the camp hours after the armistice, intentionally leaving Joey locked in his cell. Why him? He said he could not imagine. Had they heard him pray? Did they hate America and religion that much? He could not fathom such a thing.

He told me he collapsed on the dirt floor of his cell, some three or four days after he was left completely alone. He fell on the dirt floor from hunger, thirst, and dehydration. But his falling was a godsend. He spotted under his bunk, against the wall, a rusty, dented tin cup. He retrieved it; then reached as high as he could, and set it in the open cell window. He then prayed for rain. Joey said it then rained at least a little, every day, for fifteen days straight.

He sipped sparingly each day from the rusty cup. Only a third of it would fill with rainwater each day. But it saved his life.

It was on day seventeen, that he was awakened by a noise. Voices. Loud voices. And he could tell they were speaking English. In moments, there was a heavy knock on his cell door. "Anyone here?" a male voice yelled.

"Yes! Yes!" Joey responded. But was not at all sure they could hear him. His voice was so weak. He did not have the strength to get up off his bunk.

Joey slipped again into unconsciousness. Until! BAM!! BAM!! A battering ram of some sort was being slammed against the cell door.

"Stand clear!" said a voice. BAM!! BAM!! It took at least a half-dozen attempts, but Joey heard the door crash to the floor.

He struggled to open his eyes. And when he did, he saw the concerned but beaming face, of a man in uniform: the uniform of the United States Marine Corps. The marine was part of a United Nations contingent. "It was," Joey said, "the most marvelous sight ever!"

And I had to ask Joey why... WHY?... did he not contact me, or his family, as soon as he was back in American hands? And his answer pierced my heart. He said he feared that I—after his being out of touch for so long—would presume him dead. He was afraid I might have even married again. He was determined to find out such details, before contacting me.

Upon arriving in the states, he telephoned Robertson's jewelry and, without identifying himself, asked for me. When told a simple "No," he quickly hung up, fearing his imaginings were being confirmed. If I were re-married—or even engaged—he had promised himself he would move on with his life; he would never let me know he was alive. The thought still breaks my heart. Finally, he decided to arrive unannounced in Rodessa to see his parents. Who can doubt? His timing was providential.

Six months after we returned to Portsmouth, little Jo Alben and I were baptized at St. Catherine of Siena's. You may think that unimportant to the story; but it is to me.

Joey was already, because of his "forced extension" of service, in his third four-year hitch in the navy. He, of course, could have gotten his discharge immediately. But President Eisenhower (I'm told it was one of his first acts as President), signed the commission upgrading Joey to an officer. In fact, the President stair-stepped him over several ranks. He was now Lieutenant Commander Joey J. Thibodeaux, United States Navy. The President was undoubtedly aware of the heroic mission Joey and his two buddies accepted, and was unsure any of them would ever come home. In fact, so far as I know, the other two never returned.

Out of gratitude—and the fact that the navy was all he knew, or wanted anyway—Joey decided to serve out that third hitch. "If," he told me, "they can find something I'm healthy enough to do. Something useful."

They made him an aide to the Commanding Officer at Portsmouth Naval Yard. It was a desk job; not overly demanding, but he felt it important and satisfying.

However. Sadly. I did not have Joey very long. His prisoner of war years: the days, weeks, months? of beatings. The near starvation. It brought on a malnutrition which was debilitating. And I'm sorry to say, he just could not give up his cigarettes. It all took its toll. I lost him six years and three months after his return. We buried him at sea, in the Atlantic, as he had requested. I miss him so. But those six years were wonderful.

Needless to say, my dreams of being the next Ava Gardner on the 'Silver Screen' never came true. But I must admit I got a special thrill in the early '80s, when a wonderful movie star—Ronald Reagan—made it to the White

House. I am pleased that historians, by and large, seem to agree he did quite a credible job.

I never got back to college, but in 1962 Mister Robertson wanted to retire, and I got a loan to buy the store. Eight years later, I'd had enough success that I obtained a much bigger loan. I acquired a three-story building a couple of blocks away on Congress, and Thibodeaux's Department Store was born. Finally, in 2005 I sold the building and the business, to Macy's. Subsequently, they moved to 'The Mall at Fox Run', in Newington.

Jo Alben? She was a runner-up in the Miss New Hampshsire Contest, 1970. She now teaches American History at St. Anshelm's College in Manchester. She was terribly career-oriented, and never got around to giving me grandkids. But she did marry a fellow professor when she was forty-two. They commute every Sunday to mass at Corpus Christi Parish in Portsmouth, where Jo Alben is a regular lector. Then, they take me to Sunday brunch.

Two years after we returned to Portsmouth, Joey and I had a baby boy. We named him Joey James Thibodeaux Junior. I insisted. "JJ", as we call him, is now a contractor and master carpenter in Boston. He makes quite a good living, refurbishing old historic homes and buildings. He and his lovely wife Shelly drive up from Boston to join us for mass and brunch every six weeks or so; and they have given me grandkids. Twin girls! Jamie and Chloe are now enrolled in the University of New Hampshire, Durham. And they crash (Crash? I think that's what they call it), at my house at least one weekend a month. I am now Gram-ma-ma.

When I could afford it, I started looking for a house of my own. I had upgraded a time or two, to more spacious and very comfortable apartments, but I wanted a house. But I did not want a mortgage. I looked a bit on Kittery Island. (By the way, the *Sand Lance* was the last submarine built at the Naval Yard. It launched in 1969; but the place is still abuzz with good-looking sailors, as the yard does refueling, modernization, and overhaul work for the subs).

So, as I started looking for a home, I thought it might make me feel closer to Joey, if I lived in Kittery. But seeing all those wonderful, athletic young sailors walking around; they were everywhere I turned. Sorry to say, it made me more lonely for Joey than I already was. Too lonely.

So, I now live in a spacious and beautiful house near Pearl and Islington Streets; Portsmouth's historic district. It is like many houses in the city: this one built in the late 1800s; a tall, three-story wooden house with a gabled roof; a combination of Victorian, Georgian, and Federalist architecture. It's a soft, pale yellow with forest green shutters. The shingled roof matches the shutters. I had often driven by the house, and strongly admired it. The gentleman died, who had lived their for years. He was well into his nineties, quite wealthy, and had kept the place well-maintained. I have never seen the house with its paint faded, or a shabbly spot anywhere. When it came on the market, I immediately called the realtor and told him I'd take it. And, yes—I proudly paid cash for the house. No mortgage. Life is good. God has blessed.

I think often of Heavener, Oklahoma, my dear late parents, and of course, the long-departed Fred the Dog. But Portsmouth—here, close to the sea and my dear Joey. This… is home.

However. If I could find a refurbished, fully operational, '49 Ford Custom Club Coupe' in silver blue—I would buy it with cash.

Well. I am tired. It is time to end this little memoir. But I want to finish that same brief poem, with which I started:

"… a folly so reckless…

… a foolish young fling…

… a selfish indulgence…

… brings others much pain…

… but Angels in Heaven…

… protect a young love…

… and plead for Redemption…

… God's Gift from above… "

THE END

AUTHOR'S NOTE

"RUNAWAY SOUTHERN BELLE" is a work of fiction. Obviously, there are real historical figures who make appearances in the novel—Vice-President Barkley, Speaker Rayburn, and actress Vera Miles to name a few. The 1950 mission of the British marines and the USS Perch did occur.

But the main characters: Alben James Barkley of Heavener, Oklahoma, Joey James Thibodeux of Rodessa, Louisiana, and their families, exist only in the author's mind. It was easy to write a tale saying that the Vice-President had a nephew and grand-niece in Heavener, Oklahoma, that he was barely aware of. This, because it has been said that Mr. Barkley was not particularly close to some distant relatives.

I could not fail to mention that the *Southern Belle* of the Kansas City Southern Railway was indeed one of America's premier streamliners in the '40s, '50s, and '60s. I had the great privilege to ride many of the country's famous trains, but sadly, never the *Southern Belle*. The loss is mine. And the loss of so many great streamliners, is a loss for America.

Finally, I wish to thank my dear friends, R.C. "Bob" and Joyce Salmons, of Overland Park, Kansas. It was their gift of a little book: "Images of Rail: Kansas City Southern Railway", by Thad Hillis Carter, that inspired my story.

Jerry L. Minshall
Nashville, Tennessee
2019